I Won't Always Old!

by
Rachel C. Wilson

I Won't Always Old!

Library of Congress Catalog Card Number
97-62085

ISBN: 1-890306-07-X

Cover Design by Purnell H. Pettyjohn

Warwick House Publishers
720 Court Street
Lynchburg, Virginia

Dedication

This book is dedicated to my late mother, the real Ida Faye; my grandson Chad, who reminds me of El; many family members who will recognize themselves; and to the memory of my dear friend, Shirley Wayman Moore, who believed in my writing.

Acknowledgments

I appreciate the support of The Writers' Group at Sedalia Center, Big Island, Virginia, who listened and critiqued my book; Dawn Fisher, for her helpful editing; and Dr. William Young for his direction and advice.

I
Won't
Always
Old!

Always Old!

——◆——

she raised her aching body from
her stooped frame into the nearby
made her way to the door of the
the lock, and shuffled into the
vator was slow, but the handrail
confidence; if she gripped it with her strong hand
— holding her body just so — the casual hall-walker would
tell her that she looked good today. Ida Faye Dowling
Crawford was determined not to droop.

She pushed the button, bracing herself with the cane as
the elevator made its slow climb up the six floors to where
she waited. There had been a time when she had moved
through the corridor behind her — making twelve rounds
every single day, arms swinging, head held high — but that
was before... before the crippling pain, before the fluid be-
gan to swell the legs, before those unsightly elastic stock-
ings. That was before the left hand became so twisted that
she had difficulty holding a glass, before the doctor had
muttered "at your age" and "osteoperosis" and "arthritis."

Then he had the nerve to order a neck collar for me. Ida Faye
grimaced in disgust, *just like I was some old horse.* Sudden
pain shot through her back and up into her head, reminding
the white-haired lady of one of her mama's old jokes — how
"Arthir" was the worst one of those "Ritis" boys to sleep
with. Somehow, she didn't find the quip very funny any more.

1

Finally, the ancient carrier creaked to a halt, groaning as the doors pushed open like an old man's mouth snoring away on a summer day. Ida Faye hobbled into the emptiness of the dark interior and closed her eyes, trying to shut out some of the loneliness that wrapped her thoughts in misery.

The bird-eyed porch sitters stared as Ida Faye inched her way towards the parking lot. *Do not droop. Do not droop*, the old lady chanted to herself as she painfully stumbled across the concrete. Just when she thought her shaking legs would give out, she was there — standing in front of gleaming wax, reaching for the polished chrome of the sun-heated handle. Ida Faye made three attempts before she could open the car door. Thank goodness no one was close enough to see the quivering hands, to hear the sigh escaping from her lips as she grasped the trusted steering wheel and pulled herself onto the simmering vinyl. Instantly, it's warmth enveloped the pain in her legs and she melted against the plastic.

Caressing the armrest with her misshapen hand, Ida Faye felt a surge of strength push to the surface. It was almost as if the car had some special power to bring life pulsating through the spidery veins of an old woman. She was renewed! And in the silence of reflection, Ida Faye strained to catch a quiet murmur of gratitude from the shapely metal that encased her. *Thank you for appreciating me*, the sedan seemed to whisper.

And why not? Ida Faye's dearest possession had always followed her directions and never argued with her like her sister did! Anyday's destination required neither explanation nor justification. The car simply took her where she wanted to go.

A heavy sigh evaporated into the sultry air as Ida Faye gave a gentle pat to the seat back, gingerly rested her head against its firmness, and closed her eyes...

...It was 1968. She and Elmer were standing in the show-room, their smiling images mirrored in the glistening tur-quoise and glowing chrome of a brand new Chevrolet. Gig-gling, Ida Faye slid onto the seat and pushed the shining key into the switch. Elmer joined her on the passenger side, grinning from ear to ear like a kid. Hands crossed over each other as the examination began. Shiny knobs were twisted and the wipers slid across the dry windshield, boldly daring a drop of rain to mar the sparkling glass. Static blasted from front and rear speakers, and Elmer hastily turned the dial to find a station. Satisfied with the sweet strains of a George Jones melody, he announced to anyone listening, "Here we come!" and blasted the horn for effect. "Move over, we're making a left turn!" Elmer shouted as he pushed down on the signal lever.

"Hey, Pete, let's buy it!" Elmer dared Ida Faye. "Shucks, after forty-five years we can finally afford one, and even though I can't drive, this sweet baby looks like a good one to me," he laughed. "You think you still remember how to operate a motor vehicle?"

Ida Faye breathed in the smell of factory-new vinyl and turned to her husband. "I might need a little practice but I'll bet it won't take long," she crooned, her eyes shining. "Don't forget, my papa bought the first Ford in Bedford County when I was thirteen years old! I loaded that thing up with kids and headed for the fields, and when I come home, I could drive. Papa never did learn how, but he didn't waste no time in making me the official sho-fer for the family." Ida Faye clutched Elmer's hand in excitement, "Shoot, all I got to do is to get under that wheel and it'll come back to me in no time!" She smiled into Elmer's face, "Let's buy it and name it Bassy."

It was a done deal, except for the naming part — Elmer agreed to "Bassy" only after Ida Faye swore that she would not reveal its meaning to a living soul! After filling out a mountain of paperwork, the beaming couple finally stood in front of their new Chevrolet. Elmer pulled Ida Faye into his arms and whispered proudly, "This car will probably head up a big parade some day!"...

...It was a summer night and she could feel the evening cool against her face. Elmer was calling, "Hey Pete, how about a milkshake? I'll pay!" When they pulled into the drive-in, Bassy gleamed like a jewel amidst the chrome and wax of the teenagers' cars all lined up for show. Ida Faye leaned out the window and shouted into the speaker — "Two large strawberries, please!" and licked her lips in anticipation. Minutes later, she and Elmer grinned at each other over the marvelously thick concoctions, slurping loudly as they savored the last drops of sticky sweetness...

Ida Faye slowly opened her eyes and reached towards the empty seat, almost — for a moment — expecting Elmer to be there. Had it really been twenty years? It seemed like only yesterday that she had brought him home briefly after the last illness. And then, an ambulance was rushing him back to the hospital on that hot day in June. She and Bassy had followed as if they knew this would be their last trip with Elmer. Ida Faye swiped at the wetness on her cheeks as she thought about the pain of living without Elmer. Still, she had never been one to pretend that their marriage was a bed of roses. They had quarreled frequently and faced some rough times. She could still feel the agony of the Depression Years when Elmer was cut back to eight hours a week, and then had to deal with the added burden of caring for her brother and sister when they moved in because the jobs had all dried up. And the pain of struggling to maintain their dignity when payment became an impossibility and the bank repossessed their home. Yes, Ida Faye and

Elmer knew what hard times were, all right, but they knew it together, depending on each other throughout it all.

Bassy had absorbed many a tear in the years following Elmer's death as the lonely woman tried to pick up the pieces of her life; the car took on more importance as Ida Faye adjusted to being a widow. She drove to her party's headquarters to stuff envelopes for mailing and then transported friends to the polls on election day, but only if they promised to vote Democrat and did not hold her responsible for their safety in the car. Ida Faye joined a women's club and took up canasta. At ten o'clock a.m. on the first Tuesday of each month she would leave Bassy in the church parking lot, clutch her simple bag lunch, and join the women in the missionary circle for a lively discussion. Regular visits to nursing homes — her special ministry — reminded Ida Faye that it was only through God's grace that she was the visitor rather than the invalid.

Gradually she and Bassy accepted the reality of Elmer's death. His "Watch out for that car!" and cautions about her speed surfaced in her thoughts less often...

The sound of a horn interrupted Ida Faye's reveries. From deep within, a sob began to build. She felt the intense pain of separation as loneliness struggled to the surface. Only Bassy heard the mournful wail. A cloudy-eyed Ida Faye took one more look around and then pushed the handle down. Cautiously, the old lady stretched fragile legs towards the ground and steadied herself with the cane. She stood, pulled her small frame as straight as possible, and slammed the door behind her. One last time, she turned and gently tapped the surface while muttering under her breath, "You've been a good ole girl. You've been the best ole girl."

Squaring her shoulders, Ida Faye refused to meet the eyes of the porch sitters as she passed on her way to the mailbox. Unshed tears blinded her momentarily as she fumbled with the contraption a little longer than usual, trying to delay the disappointment that she always felt when the box was empty.

But wait! Here was a letter! Her dimming vision made reading it an impossibility, but it felt good just to hold the treasure in her hand. Her steps were lighter, now, as she hurried to the apartment, and then slowed down long enough to make herself a cup of tea.

Finally, Ida Faye lowered herself into the rocking chair and lay her cane on the floor beside it. Awkward fingers pulled at the envelope flap until she was able to slide her trembling hand into its folds and pull out a single sheet. Moving the paper closer to the light, she focused the magnifying glass on the tiny print and began to read:

Division of Motor Vehicles
Richmond, Virginia
June 1, 1991

Mrs. Ida Faye Crawford
Manor House Apartments
Lynchburg, Virginia 24501

Dear Ms Crawford:
We have received your driver's license and wish to thank you for relinquishing it on your 90th birthday. We congratulate you for your excellent driving record, and sincerely praise you for voluntarily submitting your permit.

Yours truly,
Verona Tate, DMV

Her head drooped in defeat. Ida Faye wept.

The Apartment

—◦—

"This apartment ain't spacious, but thank God it ain't a nursing home," Ida Faye said aloud as she turned sideways to squeeze past the utility table and into the kitchen. "I pay the rent and don't owe a dime on anything in this place!" she added. Three more steps and she was in front of the refrigerator door, her very own magnetized picture gallery. Affectionately, she touched first one and then another of the photographs.... "John, darling," she whispered to a handsome young man... "Mama, I still think of you... Elmer."

With a deep sigh, Ida Faye took the quarter turn to face the sink and cabinets where her dishes were stacked. A now familiar stab of pain shot through her arm as she stretched to reach a cup and saucer. Her shoulder ached as she lifted the partially filled kettle of water onto the stove and switched the burner to "High." While the water heated, Ida Faye retrieved a previously used tea bag from an earlier cup and carefully measured one teaspoon of sugar into the clean one. She toasted a couple of pieces of bread, spread jam to the edges, and then filled a soup bowl with All Bran topped off with a slice of banana. As she poured milk from the plastic jug, Ida Faye muttered a reluctant "Thanks!" to her daughter, Jane, for the loosened cap. She was ready to enjoy her breakfast.

Two trips later, Ida Faye took a seat at the table. She turned her face towards the painting that had graced every one of her dining room walls for forty years, and which she had committed to memory. Following the example of the old man in the painting, Ida Faye folded her hands, bowed her head, and asked God to bless her food. As she ate she looked at the things that surrounded her, things that gave her a sense of identity.

Had it really been six years since that moving day in September? She had planned ahead so that every piece of furniture could be brought in and placed exactly where she wanted it. Annie had come up from Tidewater to help, and surprisingly enough, both of her daughters had catered to her wishes without much complaining. Neither of the two girls had tried to persuade her about where to put things — *Jane doesn't like to be called a girl*, Ida Faye reflected, *but as my mother used to say, 'What she don't know won't hurt her!* — and the day had gone smoothly.

Sipping the now-cool tea, Ida Faye took a mental inventory of the room, starting with the table. It had belonged to her son-in-law, Joe, during the brief time he and Jane had separated. When Joe moved back in, the reunited couple said that Ida Faye could use it, and after Joe's death, Jane gave the table to her mother. Right beside the table was the cherished Victorian loveseat, still a good-looking piece of furniture. It had cost Ida Faye ten dollars in 1935, a small fortune. Elmer thought his wife had lost her mind to spend money on something so unneeded when they were having such a hard time making ends meet. But, she knew it was a good deal and had insisted. Now the love seat was a genuine antique, and Jane had hinted more than once that she hoped Ida Faye would leave it to her someday.

On the desk — one of the few redeemable pieces of furniture after the fire of 1929 — stood the framed pictures of her girls and their families. *I'll never forget that Easter*

Sunday if I live to be one hundred and fifty, thought Ida Faye. She and Elmer had left their five-year-old, Jane, asleep and alone in the house while they went to the Sunrise Service. Jane was fine, and she didn't even wake up 'til after they had returned. But, that very night — while the family was at church once again — someone had come up to Elmer and whispered that their house was on fire. Ida Faye, Elmer, and Jane got to the burning house just in time to see the piano fall through the living room floor. Only a few things survived. Jane found her favorite doll and didn't want to give it up. The little girl cried so pitifully that the insurance agent agreed that she could keep the doll, Geraldine, even though the porcelain face was blackened and the dress smelt horribly of wet soot. Watching the smoke curl up from the ruins, terror threatened to overwhelm Ida Faye as it came to her that the fire might have started that morning when Jane was sleeping in the house alone. It was five years before the frightened mother would leave Jane by herself again.

Shuddering at the memory, Ida Faye allowed herself a minute to reassemble her thoughts. Her poor eyes strained to make out a picture of her other daughter, Annie, and son-in-law, Bert. Photos of Jane and Joe, their two daughters and son, plus ten grandchildren filled the desk top. A tear rolled down the old woman's face as she gazed at a photo of her oldest granddaughter, Patricia, who had died of cancer. Life could be so short.

"I'd buy a new sofa if I knew I'd live another five years," Ida Faye intoned, as her eyes rested on the worn couch beside the desk. "But that's just another bit of foolishness, so I may as well forget it!" Next to the sofa stood the record player console, a gift from Elmer's sister. Whenever Ida Faye felt especially lonely, she'd get out the old LPs. Remembering how sad they could make her, she silently promised herself that she wasn't going to play them again — at least not anytime soon.

The rocking chair, a balm to her crippled body, completed the furnishings of the room. Ida Faye had bought it from the man across the hall when his family decided to move him to a nursing home, a thought that always made Ida Faye shudder in repulsion.

From the table, Ida Faye could see into the other two rooms. She focused on the blue toilet seat, a present from her granddaughter Della. "Its softness sure does feel good on the old butt on a cold winter's day!" she mused out loud. The dim outline of an attachment to her bed in the sleeping area made her groan. The rail was her symbol of helplessness — she had to use it to pull herself up and out of bed each day. Her eyes moved to the cedar chest, an old treadle sewing machine, and a chest of drawers that lined the walls of the crowded bedroom. But her favorite piece sat caddy-cornered: it was Elmer's worn armchair. Sometimes she would pretend that he was sitting with her in it.

Well, that was that! Ida Faye began the arduous task of carrying the breakfast dishes back to the kitchen. The aged eyes took in the sparse shelves holding a few special pieces of china and trinkets from the past. Brushing against the crockery churn in the corner of the kitchen, she recalled a time when she sat on the back porch of her childhood home and lifted and lowered that paddle until the rich butter came to the top.

Above the churn was the framed chart that recorded names and dates of eight generations of her family. She couldn't read the print any more, even with her magnifying glass, but Ida Faye knew the history was there. She could call out most of the names just as if she had met them personally. It was because of the chart that she had joined the

United Daughters of the American Revolution. Though she had never gone to many meetings, it made her feel good to know that she was qualified.

Ida Faye was especially proud of the framed certificate that hung beside the chart. It amused her to watch peoples' reactions when they read it and realized that she had been over seventy years old when she earned the honor. Entitled, "ORDER OF THE MASTER MULE SKINNERS OF THE GRAND CANYON TRAILS," it read:

> "Be it known to all that Ida Faye Crawford was a member of today's party on Bright Angel Trail to the Colorado River and, having faced the precipices, descended and ascended the perpendicular walls at and in the South Rim of the Grand Canyon, endured the vissitudes of this magnificent journey, and borne the whims and caprices of her gentle, faithful, educated, individualistic, long-eared mount — part horse, part jackass and all mule — named Salem, is now a member of the renowned Order of the Master Mule Skinners of the Grand Canyon Trails, with rights and privileges to boast of this accomplished feat forevermore.
>
> Issued by Fred Harvey, this 20th day of Sept., 1971. Certified to by an expert witness of the magnificent cooperation between rider and mule during the entire journey.
>
> Signed
> Dean Clevenger

Though Ida Faye's tired eyes couldn't make out the fine print, she had never forgotten the "part jackass and all mule" and she allowed that this might be an accurate description of her disposition these days. It was worth a good laugh.

Bassy

⌒⌒

*I*da Faye had just put away the last dish when she heard a knock at her door. "Coming!" she yelled as she slowly edged her way past the table, the love seat, and the sofa. "El, is that you?" she quizzed as she grasped the knob with her right hand, balanced herself, and jerked the door open. Without thinking, Ida Faye blurted out the question she'd been pondering ever since her great-grandson had called to say he was coming by, "Want me to leave you my car when I die?"

"Well, you're not planning on going anytime soon, are you?" grinned the handsome boy, giving her a big hug.

"Nope, but your grandmother keeps bringing up the subject of dying and wills and all that trash, so just thought I'd ask. To hear her talk you'd think I'm ready for my funeral right this minute. I may be too old to drive Bassy anymore but I'm not kicking the bucket yet," the old woman replied.

El's smile faded. "Lady, are you serious?"

"Course I'm serious, son. Why every last woman on my mother's side lived to be at least ninety-eight, and I'm not gonna let them beat me. I'm gonna be around for a spell."

El laughed. "I'm sure you are, but I wasn't talking about how long you'll live. I mean, are you serious about giving me the car?" he asked.

"Well, there may be a few strings attached to my offer. You'd have to promise me to take extra good care of her. You know she's not just any ole car; she's a member of the family."

"I know!" El answered, "and I would take care of her." He hesitated, "But what are the other strings?"

Ida Faye motioned for El to take a seat at the table before she answered – thoughtfully, as if she had been planning this entire offer for a long time. "Well, I need a driver to take me places," she paused for a moment, "like the store and the bank. I just don't want to be beholden to my children if I don't have to. Course, I'd pay for the gas and I'd try not to be too much of a bother to you." Curious brown eyes watched El intently. "What do you think? Are you interested?"

El's gaze never faltered. "Yeah, Lady, I think I am," he replied. "I'd like to own ole Bassy. She's a collector's item, I think, and if I ever make my fortune, I may just decide to collect cars. Bassy'd be a good start. Mom has some pretty awesome stories about that car. She's told us about the time she and Mike and Patricia and you were driving up the wrong way on the highway in Portsmouth."

"I don't know why she had to go and tell that on me, Ida Faye fumed. "I just turned around right there in the middle of the road and kept going. Then, I told your mama and them to hush up that yelling and we just went on where we was headed," Ida Faye concluded. Her tone of voice let El know that it would be better to leave the driving story alone, so he decided to change the subject.

"When are you gonna tell me how come you call her Bassy?" he appealed.

Ida Faye grinned, "Well, maybe soon if I'm sure you're gonna treat her right. Elmer and me was the only living souls that knew about that name." Ida Faye's wrinkled face turned a warm red as she mumbled, "And it don't exactly go with 'Lady,' neither."

"Aw, come on now." El grinned as he shifted to meet his great-grandmother's eyes, "You've never done anything that would change your being Lady." He continued, "Did you know that 'Lady' has saved me a lot of explanations?" asked El.

"How's that?" Ida Faye retorted.

"Well, just think about it. I have five grandmas, counting you, and all of the others want to be called 'Nanna.' So I have to say 'Nanna Green' or 'Nanna Dodd' or 'Nanna Poe' or 'Nanna Stewart.' When I say 'Lady,' there's only one." El reached across the table to pat her hand.

"There ain't but one of you, either, Rascal!" El heard the tenderness in the cracking voice. Clearing her throat, Ida Faye pushed the tears aside, "But let's get back to Bassy. Want to stroll out to the parking lot and have a look at her?"

"Sounds good to me!" El replied, as he held the chair steady for Ida Faye to stand. He stared at his grandma in admiration. *She's something else*, thought El. *Her hands are twisted and knotted and her eyesight gets worse every time I see her, and if she hasn't just replaced the batteries in her hearing aid, I have to yell to make her understand. But, I love her feisty nature and all those stories she tells! What determination!*

As they rode down in the elevator Ida Faye caught her reflection in the mirror and patted her snow white hair. "Aw shucks," she said as if she could really see herself clearly, "I forgot to put on lipstick."

"The Lady looks beautiful to me," murmered El, and instantly, a smile lit up Ida Faye's face.

When they stepped into the lobby, Ida Faye pulled on El's arm and tried to whisper — an impossible feat. She nodded in the direction of a group of women gathered on the porch.

"I can't stand them," she said. "They sit in those rocking chairs day after day and gossip. Reminds me of a row of buzzards like my brothers used to shoot off the fence. I hope the good Lord takes me away from here before I'm ever tempted to join them!"

El smiled as Ida Faye took his arm. He noted that she "good mornin'ed" the porch sitters as they passed. He wondered if she would ever give in and join the old birds, now that she was no longer able to drive. He was reminded of earlier days when Ida Faye drove and he rode along to help her get groceries. Sometimes, as they were leaving the apartment, the old widow would intentionally wander into the handicapped parking area as if looking for her car. Then, when she knew she had the attention of the rockers, she would shout to El, "Now just what am I doing in this lot?" and laugh at her own joke. Generally, guilt would prompt her to swing the car back around to the porch to ask if she could get anything from the store for anyone.

"One of these days I'm gonna stop and pull an old trick on them," Ida Faye's voice broke into El's recollections. "The one Preacher Watson used so we'd all come to church on Sunday night. Why I could pack this porch with curiosity seekers!" gloated Ida Faye.

"And what did the preacher do?" asked El.

"Well, one Sunday morning he told the congregation they'd better come to church services that night, because he was going to show something they'd never seen before and would never see again after the service.

"Naturally, we were all as curious as the next one, so we packed the place. He kept us in suspense for a long time — he was good at that, don't you know. Had us sing lots of hymns, prayed extra long and then gave a sermon that lasted almost an hour. Everybody was tired and some was yawning, thinking 'bout they had to get up early the next morning to go to work. But we won't about to budge 'til Preacher kept his promise.

"Then, at the very last thing, near the end of the sermon — like it was something that had slipped his mind — and with the most innocent look on his face, he gave us a big grin. Said he'd almost forgot his promise. Everybody woke up on that one and we probably all leaned forward so as not to miss a word. And you know what he did?" asked Ida Faye.

"No, what?" El smiled at the excitement mirrored on his great-grandmother's face.

"That old jokester just pulled an apple out of his pocket and held it up high. 'See,' he said. 'Here's an apple that you never saw before. Right?' We all had to agree that we hadn't seen it before that very minute.

"He bit into that apple and ate everything down to the core. 'And now, you'll never see it again,' he finished, and sat down. Course we knew then that the joke was on us — and only because we was so crazy about Preacher Watson, we just laughed it off."

"Lady, I would not recommend that you try that on your neighbors," El admonished. "You may not be Preacher Watson to them!"

As they crossed the parking area, El thought about the day that Lady and Elmer had bought Bassy — Ida Faye had told him often enough! And he'd heard story after story about Elmer, Ida Faye, and Bassy — told just as if Bassy were a person, too. And even though he had never known his great-granddaddy Elmer, the young man had strong impressions of Ida Faye's husband, mostly because of Lady's reminiscences repeated over and over ever since he was a 'chap,' as Ida Faye liked to say — later.

El smiled as he watched Ida Faye fumble inside her blouse front and pull out a long chain from around her neck. "No wonder she droops," he thought, as he counted at least five keys. He waited patiently for his grandma to unlock the car door and offered a steadying arm as she slowly eased onto the driver's seat and gripped the steering wheel. Then, before El had time to get in and settle down, Lady had turned the key in the switch. "If Bassy's motor is still running, then so is mine," Ida Faye emphasized, and they laughed together.

El had forgotten just how good the car looked. The black upholstery didn't have a blemish as far as he could tell. "The original seat belts look as though they have scarcely been used and the skinny steering wheel won't bother me at all," El speculated. Ida Faye didn't object when he turned on the radio. It sounded good! He knew that Bassy had been painted no more than two months ago, restored to the original color. As always, she was spotlessly clean. Excitement built within El as he examined the car in a different light. *I don't want to wait for Lady to die to own this baby!* He asked on impulse, "Lady, would you consider giving me the car now? I'd take good care of her and run you wherever you need to go!"

Ida Faye ignored the question. She instructed El to open the glove compartment. "I'll need to think about that proposition for awhile," she reluctantly replied. "For now, I have something I want to show you." She pointed toward the open cubicle, "See a cigar box in there?" El nodded. "Take it out — carefully, now — and look inside."

El did as he was told. As he raised the lid on the box the faint smell of lavender filled the car. Hundreds of small purple blossoms covered the tissue paper-wrapped contents. Being very careful not to spill any of this shared treasure, El gingerly separated the folds, half expecting to discover the sparkle of gold beneath the yellowed shroud.

Spirits

— ◆ —

"Look in there and take out something," Ida Faye commanded El. "Don't mess 'em up, be careful. They won't break, so you don't have to worry 'bout that. Ain't worth any money really, but that's my memory box, so they're valuable to me." Ida Faye's eyes never left the treasures. "I like to carry them around with me and Bassy — sorta makes us more kin! Elmer used to keep stuff in that very box." The old lady's sentiments were obvious, "Maybe you'll want to keep your own box of memories, too, when you get this car. 'Twould only be fitting."

At that moment, El couldn't imagine what he would carry around for memories, but he sure hadn't missed Ida Faye's "when you get this car." He half-heartedly remarked, "Yeah, that would be cool!" and pulled out a faded paper napkin. Fingering the old paper, El quizzed his great-grandmother, "Why's this in here, Lady?"

"Turn it over and you'll see," was the reply.

"Oh, it's Mama's wedding napkin." He read from the corner, 'Our Wedding Day, Della and Ken, June 30,1970.' Daddy just took her out last week to celebrate their twenty-second anniversary. How about this!"

"Humph," snorted Ida Faye. "'Twas your Daddy's wedding, too, and I blamed him for all the drinking that went on. I'm sure he was the one who taught your mama how. She sure as shooting didn't learn it growing up in my Jane's house. Matter of fact, Ken was the one who gave the first drink to your grandma and grandpa. There sure won't no likker in our house. We raised up our kids to know right from wrong, and they never saw us take a drink, no siree Bob," Ida Faye's knotted fingers punctuated the air for emphasis, "I stayed mad about that wedding for a long time!"

"Up 'til then, I didn't even know your mama would take a drink," continued Ida Faye, "and after I saw it happen I didn't sleep a wink all night. And I'd bet a dollar your granddad won't stone sober when he had those two wrecks, either! Course I didn't think any such thing when it happened."

"Whoa, Lady," El interrupted, "Slow down. You've lost me! What are you talking about — all the drinking and the wrecks?" he continued.

"Why, the two Joe had on the day of the wedding practice, of course," exclaimed Ida Faye. "You mean they ain't told you about them?" she gasped in disbelief.

"Well, maybe they did," El gave a nonchalant shrug, "but I don't remember, so you just go ahead and tell me again!"

"Just makes me more certain that I was right," Ida Faye fumed. "If they won't hiding something then you'd a heard it and remembered it. It's not the kind of story you forget when it's about your mama," declared Ida Faye. She took a deep breath. "When the first one happened, your granddaddy Joe was on the way to pick up his monkey suit for the wedding."

"Monkey suit?" laughed El.

"Yeah, a tux-e-do," Ida Faye frowned at the teasing. "He was downtown 'bout four o'clock, heading for the store where you rent them and didn't stop for a red light. A taxicab came roaring through and hit him broadside. Course, we all knew he won't happy 'bout the wedding. It won't that he didn't like your daddy, but he had his hopes set on your mama bein' a great pipe organ player and the romance put a stop to that. Joe said he was just thinking 'bout how good she played when he was hit. He was lucky that he didn't get hurt," concluded Ida Faye. "It dented up his big car," she snickered, "and he didn't like that one bit! Joe never wanted to be driving around in no banged up car, no siree, Bob!"

"I'll bet my grandmother got mad about that," El intoned.

"She didn't know anything 'bout it, at least not 'til that night," Ida Faye went on. "At 'bout seven o'clock Jane and Joe was driving to the church to practice the wedding and he was just starting to tell her 'bout it when she yelled. Here comes another car, and danged if it didn't crash into the other side of your granddaddy's Cadillac." Ida Faye was obviously enjoying herself, but she waited for El's "Well, go on!" before she continued.

"The rest of us was already at the church, wondering where the two of them was. The preacher was getting antsy, and your mama won't happy neither. When they got the phone call we all piled into separate cars and went to see." Ida Faye hooted, "Boy, was it a speckticle. There was your granddaddy trying to explain to the officer that the car was just hit on one side and hating to say he had the four o'clock wreck that had messed up the other side. Your grandmother Jane was mad as a hornet 'cause she had figured out that Joe was at fault for both wrecks. And there we all was, dressed up fit to kill. I had on a pretty long pink dress with ruffles around the neck — the same one I'm saving to be buried in. Everybody looked mighty fine." Ida Faye wiped tears from her eyes and dropped her voice to a solemn tone. "The policeman said it was the best dressed wreck he'd ever had."

"Probably was," chuckled El. "What did the policeman do to Granddaddy?"

"Wrote a ticket and told him to be in court the next week. Joe got hisself a lawyer 'cause he was scared he'd lose his permit. I think he had to pay 'bout a hundred dollars. I remember he had to drive careful for a long time after that," Ida Faye concluded.

"Okay, so that explains why you were so mad about the wedding. But, you got over it, didn't you?" asked El.

Ida Faye nodded. "Well, yes I did — after awhile — but that won't the end of the wedding story. At the party after the practice they had what they kept calling an open bar, and I saw with my own eyes your mama and your daddy drinking. And if that won't enough, I saw your grandmothers and granddads, your aunts and uncles and even my preacher and his wife boozing. It was disgusting!" the old lady grimmaced. "My own daughter Jane had the nerve to ask me if I wanted a drink. I lit into her like you wouldn't believe. I told her if I'd a known there was gonna be all that drinking, I woulda never let her use that white milk glass bowl that belonged to Mama. It was on Mama and Papa's wedding table when they were married back in 1894. It was plum sacreligious to use that bowl where there was likker." Lady shook her head in disgust. "I couldn't believe Jane had done that."

El didn't have any problems believing it, but kept quiet as Ida Faye continued, "Well, you can bet I didn't sleep a wink all that night, and if that won't enough, they had to go and have champagne at the wedding reception in the church. I thought I'd die! I sure hope you don't never take a drink, El!" she charged. "I've seen too much of it in my lifetime. All of my brothers drank, but they hid it so well that Papa never knew. Good thing, too, cause he'd a horse whipped them, no matter how big they was. Papa never took a drink his whole life.

"After Papa died, Mama moved to Roanoke and took in boarders. She got really good at worming out confessions when she thought they'd been drinking. One time my brother Harold snuck in the front door, planning to make a bee-line to his room before Mama could see him, but he won't a bee and Mama was waiting like an eagle ready to pounce." Ida Faye's eyes took on a distant look, as if she was standing in that hall so long ago! "When Mama accused him, he tried to draw hisself up nice and tall and talk proper. 'No, I- ain't-a-been-a-drinking,' he said very slowly. 'I-was -just-down-to-the-cor-ner-and-I-had-a fith-thand-wich-and-that's-what-you-smell!'

"Mama was stone silent, then she got right behind him, and followed him to his room, step by step. In a minute, out she came, with a bottle of likker tight in her hands. She uttered a 'Humph!' and went straight to the kitchen sink and poured it down the drain. Harold found hisself another place to live. After that, if we really wanted to get his goat, we'd ask him if he'd like a fith sandwich!

"The story of my brother Royal and of Brother Otis won't funny, though." Ida shook her head in dismay. "They couldn't let the stuff alone and it killed both of them — after it had ruined their lives anyway. Royal lost his sweetheart 'cause he wouldn't give up the bottle, and Otis lost his wife and child. The two of them drank theirselves right through one Christmas, a smoking and all, and while Royal was asleep on the sofa, one of them dropped a cigarette and the settee burned up and so did Royal!"

"Oh, Lady, how awful," El gasped. "How long ago was that?"

"It was the Christmas of 1952 — one I'll never forget," Ida Faye replied, sadness etched across her face.

"I'm sure you won't," said El. He hesitated, almost afraid to ask... "What happened to Otis?"

"He was hurting an awful lot, so he straightened hisself out for a long time, sober as a judge. He wouldn't admit that he had a drinking problem. Then one day he just hopped on the bus and got off at its first stop, bought hisself some rum and went to an old hotel. Five days after that they found him dead in his rented room."

"What a horrible way to die," El groaned, "and to lose your brothers. It's no wonder that you hate it so!"

"I've shed many a tear over alkihol," Ida Faye muttered, "and so maybe you can understand why it took me awhile to get over the wedding." Her voice grew stronger, "After I finally calmed down, the family began to let me see them drinking, and when I saw they could do it and not fall out on the floor dead drunk, I won't so bad about it. I even brought out the bottle that Elmer had always kept in the cedar chest. The factory gave it to him one Christmas," Ida Faye admitted sheepishly.

"You mean you started drinking?" El's mouth opened in astonishment.

"Nope, leastways not then," she replied. "But one winter when Bert had a leave from the army and him and your great aunt Annie came from where he was stationed in Georgia, I fixed him a hot toddy from the cedar chest bourbon and his cold cleared up just like that! It won't long before Elmer said he had a cold and I felt a little sniffle myself, so I fixed two more."

"Uh huh, so my great-granddaddy did drink after all," accused El.

"Nope, not except for that one time," replied Ida Faye. "He used to say that beer reminded him of horse pee. My papa didn't drink neither. He always kept a bottle of 'Spirits' as he called it, but that was so he could add it to camphor and make camphorated oil."

"Camphorated oil!" El interjected. "What in the world is that?"

"Oh, everybody had to have camphorated oil," Ida Faye replied sagely. "It was used for everything. You rubbed it on you if you had an ache or if a bug bit you. We used to laugh and say it won't the oil that cured you but the terrible smell. That stuff really stunk! But the worst thing I remember about it was the night that I had to rub it on a dead baby," said Ida Faye.

"You what?" exclaimed El.

"You heard me right. I was fourteen and the Jacob's new baby had died just a few hours after it was born. I remember it was so tiny. Mama made a little dress for her to be buried in, and it would have fit my doll, it was so small. Anyway, in those days you always had to have somebody sit up all night with a corpse. Well, Mama had planned to sit up with two of the Jacob boys, but she was so tuckered out from helping cook and clean up their house for the funeral that she made me do it in her place. I'd sat up before, but Mama had always been there, so I was scared. Then when she told me that I would have to rub the baby's face with camphorated oil every hour all night long, I just about passed out. I knew better than to tell Mama I won't gonna do it, though,"

"That's gross!" said El. "Why in the world would you have to rub anything on the face of a corpse?"

"Oh, that had to be done to keep some color in her so she wouldn't look so pale for the burial," Ida Faye answered matter-of-factly. "But it gave me the heebie-jeebies. For a long time after that night I would wake up in a cold sweat remembering the way that baby's face felt."

"Gosh," said El. "That's more than enough to make anybody hate 'spirits'!"

"Took a long time for me to change," Ida Faye admitted. "Others changed too, though. Everybody stopped hiding. Your grandma came right out in the open and drank in front of me. After a few years she started asking me if I wanted a glass of wine. Course I said 'No' for 'bout twenty years, and they thought that was a permanent answer so they stopped asking me," chuckled Ida Faye. "Anyway, when I was eighty years old, Jane and Annie gave me a big birthday party and invited about one hundred people. It was a fine affair."

"Oh yeah, I think I remember that party. I couldn't have been any more than six or seven years old," El interrupted.

As if she hadn't heard him, Ida Faye kept on. "They knew better than to try and make it a surprise. One day while they was planning, I just matter-of-factly asked if they was gonna serve any 'spirits.' They hemmed and hawed and finally said they was planning two punch bowls: one 'with' and one 'without,' was the way they put it.

"Well, on the day of the party I was all gussied up, and there was a mob of people all jammed into the house. Your mama was pouring the punch from the 'with' bowl, and nice and loud, so everybody could hear me, I just said, 'I believe I'll lift my spirits and have some of Della's punch.' She grinned but didn't say a word. When she handed me the cup I winked at her."

"Lady, you're something else," El grinned.

"Ain't I though?" was the smug reply. "Enough of this. You trade places with me and drive YOUR new old car to the store. I want to buy a bottle of wine. I like to keep a little on hand, just in case," winked a mischievous Ida Faye.

Honeymoon

~—~

"A lucky penny," exclaimed El as he pulled it from the cigar box. The copper disc barely fit into his palm. On its surface he could see the outline of an Indian woman wearing a headdress. The words LUCKY PENNY were inscribed above the date — 1922. The other side of the coin revealed a likeness of the United States capitol, and El read aloud, "Souvenir of Washington, D.C." He raised his eyes to meet those of his great grandmother. "I guess it's time for another story," he invited.

"Elmer bought that when we was on our honeymoon," Ida Faye grinned. "Since it was the only one in the shop, he thought it was a good sign for our marriage. Course I knew he was worried about the little cry I had on our wedding night."

"You cried on your wedding night?" El figured that was a risky question, but it didn't keep him from asking.

"Yes, well, I did. I was sitting on Elmer's lap and I won't tell you the rest," she snickered, "but all of a sudden I was scared, like there was something bad about me being there with Elmer like that. It was crazy, but I just couldn't help it. Before I knew it I was bawling. Course, that upset Elmer, my crying and all. Anyway, I was finally able to tell him what was troubling me, and when he said what he did, I burst out laughing."

"What did he say, Lady?" quizzed El — he could almost picture the scene.

Ida Faye lowered her voice, "Elmer said, just as serious as you please, 'Well Pete, the preacher said we could.' We both got to laughing so hard we nearly busted. Anyway, I knew that bothered Elmer even though he didn't say another word about it. So, I won't surprised when he thought he ought to buy a good luck piece for us.

"We hadn't planned on getting married so soon," she continued. "Just knew each other eight months. Course, after going with John for six years and not getting to marry him made me know a long romance won't going to guarantee nothing. My landlady and Mama was pushing Elmer and me."

"Why would your landlady care? Didn't you pay your board on time?" teased El.

"In those days I paid everything I owed, right when it was due, young man," Ida Faye said sharply. "It won't until the Depression came along and nearly killed us that I had a taste of not being able to pay on time."

El was instantly contrite, "Oh, Lady, I was just kidding. Seriously though, what did your landlady have to do with your getting married?"

"It goes like this," Ida Faye smiled, "Mrs. Bethel — the landlady — was going up north to stay with her daughter who was having a baby, don't you know. She was going to be gone about a month, and Mama said it wouldn't be fitting for me to stay in the house alone, that people would talk and think I wasn't a nice girl. Course, I guess it would have been all right if I stayed there and didn't have any dates during that time, but Mama knew that won't likely. Anyway, Mama never did trust me very much, especially when it came to men. That's why I didn't marry John."

"Whoa, Lady! This is getting complicated," El sighed. "Now back up for a minute. Who was John?"

"He was my old boyfriend," Ida Faye replied. "He's dead now. I'll show you his picture sometime. Elmer was sure jealous of him! Course that don't have a thing to do with my honeymoon," she fussed.

"Well, I can see that you're going to have another story for me later on, but go ahead and finish telling me about the honeymoon in D.C.," El laughed.

"Never thought I'd be going to Washington, D.C. on my honeymoon, much less staying at the Willard Hotel. Why the Vice-President of the United States was staying there at the same time as we was there. We saw him and Mrs. Coolidge one day."

"No kidding! You mean that Calvin Coolidge was there? Are you sure that was who you really saw?" El asked in disbelief.

"Well, for one thing, I'd seen him once before!" said Ida Faye proudly. "I drove Mama and Papa to Bedford City when Calvin Coolidge gave the dedication speech when they opened the big Elks Home. I sure remember it, 'cause I had a flat tire on the way and got my hands all dirty helping change it. By the time we arrived at the big celebration, Mr. Coolidge had finished speaking and was shaking hands. I rushed up and stuck out my hand and then turned a hundred shades of red when I saw that it had grease on it. I know he saw it, too, but he acted like it was as clean as the next one and told me he was glad to make my acquaintance."

El could see the excitement in Ida Faye's face. "Gosh, Lady, that's impressive!" he applauded. "And then you saw him again at the Willard."

"Sure did," Ida Faye replied. "He was talking to the man at the hotel desk, and we was standing right behind him. We heard the clerk call him Mr. Coolidge and I told the Vice-President I was glad to see him again, but I don't think he recognized me. At least he didn't act like he did. Elmer was tickled to death though, me speaking to the Vice-President of the United States like that!" Ida Faye chortled to herself, then quickly turned back to matters at hand.

"Anyway, to get on with the story, we woulda never been in that grand hotel if Elmer had been paying for it. Couldn't afford it. But my brother, Audie, gave us the trip for a wedding present. Guess it didn't hurt his pocketbook too much, being that he was a lawyer. He met us at the train station, said he had a taxi waiting and they was expecting us at the hotel.

"Audie always was a great one for planning every single detail. He used to write a dozen letters before he came to see us, trying to plan how we'd spend every minute — even down to what we'd have to eat if we went on a picnic. He always liked to do hotshot stuff and impress people, too." Ida Faye spoke with disgust. "He would brag about how he went to France to serve in the World War and how he was on the same boat as General Pershing. What he never told was how he got dysentery on the way over, went right straight to the hospital after he got there, and was discharged and sent home the minute his bowels got straight."

El laughed but Ida Faye kept right on going. "He always wanted to act like he was big. I bet I heard the story 'bout Harry Truman a hundred times, at least, and Audie won't even no Democrat, neither!"

"Harry Truman?" El's eyebrows shot up in surprise.

"Oh, Audie declared he was at a big cocktail party at the May-flower Hotel — I remember that name — and said the waiter had a silver tray full of drinks and went right past Senator Truman to the next person. Audie said that the senator just leaned over in his chair and reached up high to the tray and took two drinks off it! Course, then, all Audie could say was that Harry Truman did that cause he was a

Democrat and a country boy. I reminded that brother of mine that he was just a country boy himself! Reckon he didn't like that too much," Ida said with a snort.

"Lady, you know you're awful, don't you?" El stated.

"Depends on who's asking," came the sharp retort. "Well, that Audie had a lot of what I always called false pride. I remember how he nearly died of embarrassment when he found out that Mama — she was visiting them in Washington — had gone to the post office and asked for some NRA stamps to mail letters with."

"Wait a minute," El interrupted in disbelief, "You mean the National Rifle Association was around then?"

"No, El," Ida Faye exclaimed in exasperation. "The NRA was one of them special programs that Franklin D. Roosevelt started when he was President. I think the R stood for recover, or something like that."

Remembering his U.S. history, El realized Ida Faye was talking about the National Recovery Act but he just let it ride. No need to say anything, because his great-grandmother was back to the honeymoon, once again.

"Anyway, Audie had a hard time getting us out of that Union Station. I nearly broke my neck off looking at all the fancy statues and columns and things. Never saw so much marble in all my life. The only other place I had ever noticed it was when we went to buy a tombstone for Charles. Never thought I'd be thinking marble was pretty!"

Elmer knew his question would detour the honeymoon story once more, but he asked it anyway. "Who was Charles?"

Ida Faye looked at El in surprise, "Why, he was my baby brother, didn't you know that?" El's blank look said it all. Ida Faye kept on talking, "He died with the scarlet fever when he was three years old. I can just barely remember him so we must have waited a long time before we bought the gravestone, cause I can remember going to Bedford City with Mama and Papa to get that. It was spooky and scary, even though they kept saying won't nobody buried there. I touched a piece of marble and it was as cold as death. So I was surprised at myself when I was a-standing in that Union Station thinking it was nice to look at."

Subconsciously, El looked at his watch and was reminded once again that the job he had taken on was going to consume far more time than he had anticipated. But he figured it would be worth it — if his patience would just hold out. Besides, he did enjoy the stories.

Ida Faye paused in her discourse, "Did I tell you about the wedding?"

El surpressed a groan and slowly shook his head from side to side. "Don't think so." Ida Faye continued.

"Anyway, Elmer and I was married at his Uncle Charlie and Aunt Mae's house. Mama came down from up in the country, but Papa couldn't leave the store. Victor and Lillian, they was our best friends, stood up with us. Preacher Watson got it in his head that they was the ones who was gonna get married, so we had to keep reminding him that it was us. We teased Elmer about how much money he paid the preacher, 'cause we heard Mr. Watson ask Elmer in a loud voice, 'Well Elmer, HOW MUCH DO YOU THINK SHE'S WORTH?' Afterwards Aunt Mae had a little wedding supper.

"I guess we created a little excitement at the old Lynchburg depot. Any fool could tell we was just married. I was wearing an 'ensemble' as they called it. It was blue velvet and cost me sixty-five dollars. The hat itself woulda made people look. On top of the brim sat a big bluebird. We had a milliner at Almond's make it special for me. You know I worked there. I have a picture of me in that outfit. It won't actually made on the day of the wedding, 'bout a week later, as a matter of fact, when I wore it up to the country, but I still call it my wedding picture."

Ida Faye closed her eyes as she visualized herself as a bride. Immodestly she admitted that she had looked like something straight out of a fashion show. She remembered the softness of the brocaded sleeves and how the skirt had hit her at mid-calf and was trimmed, just above the hem, with three rows of satin ribbon. Oh, it had been worth all the money just to fasten the embroidered belt which brought the sides of her cape together across her hips. She had pondered over whether to put on the cameo pin but had convinced herself that even though she might not ought to wear a gift from an old sweetheart, it would add a touch of elegance to the outfit. She had worn Elmer's wedding gift, a fox furpiece, for traveling. She knew it hadn't been easy for him to come up with the $125 it cost and was proud that he bought it just for her.

"Elmer looked splendid too, in his gray serge suit," she went on. "We both was still brushing the rice off when we started down the long stairs to the tracks. The train left at six o'clock that night and it pulled into the Washington station at 12:30 in the morning. Even though I was tired, I still remember that I felt just grand when the conductor put out the little stool, tipped his hat to me, and reached up and took my arm as I got off."

"Weren't you the least bit scared, Lady, being a girl from such a small place and going to the big city and everything?" quizzed El.

"Yeah, I was, but we was lucky. Because we was traveling so late and had already had the wedding supper, we didn't need to go in the dining car and worry about using the right fork and all that. Then, when we got to the Union station there won't hardly nobody around to see us gawking. The hotel lobby was empty, and Elmer and me just sat on the leather sofa while Audie signed the book and took care of things. I did blush, though, when the man carrying our bags asked me if I was Mrs. Crawford." She paused as if in deep thought, "Then I did a little work on my mind and I decided that I was gonna start acting like I was used to fine things. So, me and Elmer just followed the man down that 'Peacock Alley' is what I think they called the fancy hallway, and I acted like I owned it. I could see myself in them mirrors as we walked past gold cabinets and velvet sofas and palm trees to the elevator.

"Our room was on the eighth floor. When I saw the flowers and a silver teapot and two china cups, I remember thinking this couldn't be happening to Ida Fay Dowling from Bedford County, Virginia, but it sure enough was! If you'd seen me then, you'd know I won't always old!"

El nodded in agreement, "I believe you! I know you must have been a beautiful bride, and your honeymoon was surely impressive," he said. "I guess this is where you're gonna stop though... right?"

"No reason to," Ida Faye took a deep breath and belted out, "Ain't nothing I'm ashamed of. Course, you know I'm not gonna tell you 'bout the personal things that happen on a honeymoon, but there's lots more I can say!" was the reply.

El imagined that his great-grandmother would have told some spicy things with the least bit of encouragement but decided he wasn't quite ready for that. So he just kept quiet.

"I convinced Elmer to order breakfast in the room the next morning. Might as well continue to act like this was the way we lived. But we was both nervous while the waiter was in the room, and I bet he could tell we had never done this before. I kept on putting on airs for Elmer, after the waiter left, and he nearly died laughing when I dipped my fancy negligee sleeve right smack into the orange juice. He repeated that old saying about how you can take a country girl to the city but you can't take the country out of her.

"After breakfast we went across the street to the big department store, Garfinkle's. Elmer said, as we walked through, that we could put old Almond's Dry Goods in it about twelve times and then have room to spare. He was a big tease in those days when we didn't hardly have a care in the world. I bought a white linen handkerchief just so I could say I had bought something at Garfinkle's.

"After that we went walking, if you can call it that. It was more like we stood still with all that traffic that just kept stopping, and both me and Elmer would say, 'I never saw anything to beat it!' over and over again. There was electric streetcars, horse-drawn carriages, cars, bicycles, and the stop signals. Now they was a real curiosity! If Elmer hadn't pushed me, I might still be standing one block away from the Willard, watching a policeman direct traffic. He was under a big umbrella out in the middle of the streets, with everything roaring by, turning some contraption by hand so that the cars could see when they were to stop and go. Course, later on, when electric signs came along, it won't nothing, but back then — in 1922 — it was something to behold!

"I've been to Washington since then, but it never seemed the same. Take the Lincoln Memorial, for instance. It was brand new and didn't have all those extra steps and sidewalks like it does now. Elmer and me walked up those seventeen marble steps, counting them out loud, and what do you know. Perched on Mr. Lincoln's knee was a real live pigeon, looking like he was a part of the statue. I was reading the Gettysburg address from the wall. I had to learn that by heart when I was in school. Elmer came over to where I was standing and pulled me away, said he had something amazing to show me. 'Look at that,' he said. 'I can't believe it! I wish my Uncle Bill was here.' And then he told me what he was talking about. Lincoln's left hand formed the letter 'A' in sign language and the right one was in the position for 'L.' Abraham Lincoln! Even though I didn't know Elmer's Uncle Bill or why Elmer wished he was there, the look on Elmer's face made me wish that his Uncle Bill could see it, too!" Ida Faye paused to catch her breath, and El seized the opportunity to jump in before she got started again.

"Wow, Lady, that is some story! But I've got to soon get going. Can I please take you by the bank, now? I believe that's all you said you needed me to do today." El tried to keep his voice light so that Ida Faye wouldn't be insulted by his impatience.

"Course you can, son," an undaunted Lady continued, "I'll finish up by telling you that we stayed in Washington three days and then Audie took us to the station, bought us a sandwich, put us on the train, and we came back home, where we moved into an apartment. Now, just let me get my pocketbook and we'll be on our way."

The trip to the bank was much shorter than the stay, and El soon safely deposited Ida Faye back in the apartment, leaving her with a big hug. Once again the old lady was alone and in her rocking chair. For a short while Ida Faye's thoughts turned to her honeymoon. Closing her eyes she could see again the pink frilly nightgown and negligee. She smiled as she remembered how embarrassed Elmer had been when he tried to take them off and got the ribbons all in a tangle. He was awkward in his love making and his hands were rough on her smooth skin, but then — and in all the years to come — she never questioned that he loved her.

Elmer

———

$\mathcal{I}$t was on Thursday that Ida Faye told the story of Elmer. El had pulled a faded snapshot from the cigar box and asked her about it. The following Monday, El read his paper to the writing class:

Elmer Eugene Crawford was named after his father but the only experiences the two had shared were told to Elmer: his father had died of pneumonia in 1902 when Elmer was only two years old. Mrs. Crawford was left with four children, no money, few possessions, and no marketable skills other than sewing. Each day was a struggle just to survive. Elmer was always hungry, mainly because he felt an inner compulsion to be sure that his sisters and brother got what they wanted before he put food on his own plate. Brother Arthur saw this as a weakness and took advantage of it often.

During Elmer's first five years of life, he rarely heard his dead father mentioned except in warning. Each child was told not to touch the Bible that had belonged to their dead father. Elmer had ignored the admonishment only once.

His mother was working feverishly on a nearly completed quilt. She frantically searched the bottom of her scrap bag trying to find enough matching pieces to complete the design. Once again she was going to have to substitute other colors in the bottom row. The quilt would bring in less money.

Her preoccupation gave Elmer the moment he had been waiting for — he slipped the book off the table and took it to the bedroom that he shared with Arthur. The young boy was so absorbed in looking at the picture of a smiling, bearded man with children on his lap that he didn't hear his mother's footsteps until she was right over him. The enraged woman snatched the Bible from his small hands and slapped his face. "You ever touch that Bible again and I'll give you the whuppin' of your life!" she yelled.

Ella Crawford hadn't known what to do with the Bible when Gene died. She'd never taken any stock in reading it herself. She had more important things to do. Not so with Gene. He had quoted it all the time — 'Be sure your sins will find you out' — or one that said something about 'whoever believes in him shall have eternal life.' She had a hard enough time dealing with this life, much less worry about another one. Besides, Gene's high and mighty attitude had somehow made her feel cheap. And though she had not shared her husband's beliefs, Ella was afraid to get rid of the Bible. She might be punished by Gene's God.

Elmer did not remember how old he was when they took his two sisters away and put them in an orphanage. He was especially anxious about Louise because she was a deaf mute. Would there be anyone other than her sister, Charlotte, in the orphanage to use sign language with Louise? It saddened him to think of not being able to take up for her when others called her deaf and dumb.

Elmer realized that the reduced size of the family would mean that there was a little bit more to eat. And, when the Army folks came by in those funny-looking uniforms to see if the Crawfords wanted a basket of food, maybe they could sometimes say, "No, thank you, we don't need any."

The older son did all he could to help out. When he was seven, his mother scraped together enough money to buy some newspapers for him to sell on the Richmond streets. Elmer stood on a nearby corner and called out, "Get your morning paper! Three cents!" He would run home as soon as the last one was sold, drop the money in a jar, get his lunch pail and books, and race the few blocks to school. His mother would count out enough coins to pay for the next day's supply of papers and use the profit to supplement her pitiful earnings. Though he loved school, and especially the warmth and friendliness of his teacher, Miss Jones, Elmer fought to stay awake most days. The early morning excursions to the news office and then to his selling post left the small boy so sleepy that it often took a gentle nudge to remind him to pay attention in class.

He wished his mother would smile at him sometimes. She and his brother, Arthur, laughed when they were together. Elmer felt left out. In fact, his mother did all kinds of things with Arthur! Shame crept over him for thinking that; after all, it was his fault that Arthur was crippled. He had been taking care of the little boy on the day of the accident. Elmer didn't even know that the gun was in the closet, until he heard the shot and saw Arthur's mangled foot.

By the time Elmer had finished third grade, he was selling evening papers, as well as taking care of a rather extensive trade in the morning. He moved to a different corner, and by the middle of that summer he had established a clientele of regulars, many of whom called him by name. These customers represented a different world for Elmer. They treated him with kindness. Though his limited vocabulary did not include the word "dignity," the young man liked what he felt during the early morning encounters.

It was that same summer that he noticed that Walter Balewe, from down the street, was spending a lot of time at the Crawford house. It was pleasant to see his mother's smiles, even though these were usually directed at Walter. But there were other changes, too — ones that worried Elmer.

His mother had taken to smoking since she and Walter became so friendly. She would sit beside the man and watch as he made a big event of rolling a cigarette. First, with his left hand Walter would pull a small bag of tobacco from his pocket, holding it up as if it were a treasure just discovered. Then, he would release the pouch's drawstring with his two index fingers and gently shake a small amount of the contents onto a piece of white tissue paper that lay flat in his right palm. After pulling the drawstring closed with his teeth, Walter deftly rolled the tobacco-filled paper into a slender cylinder, licked the edges to seal it, tamped it on the table, and handed it to Ella. With a flourish he whipped out a match, found a striking surface, and held the flame to the tip of the cigarette. The scenario always ended with Ella inhaling deeply, then gently blowing some smoke into Walter's face. The two of them would laugh.

Although he didn't actually see Walter drinking, Elmer was often aware of the smell of alcohol on his breath. He could tell it, too, in the way Walter began to make little playful jabs at him, inviting — and ultimately provoking — Elmer to "See how hard you can punch me in the gut!" Sometimes, when the odor of liquor was very strong, Walter would call him "Big Shot" and poke at him. Then he would put an arm around Ella and say, "Now ain't that right, Babe?" and she would nod her head and giggle.

On Elmer's ninth birthday, Ella informed her son that she and Walter were getting married and that Elmer was going up in the country to live with his grandparents. The following Saturday, with most of his belongings packed into a shabby suitcase, the young boy's mother escorted him to the bus station and blew him a kiss as the bus rolled out of the station. Except for the hollow feeling in the pit of his stomach, Elmer's attitude stayed the same. He remembered his grandparents only vaguely — having seen them on one occasion — but he accepted this move as a part of his circumstances.

Life in the country with two people who adored their grandson was like what he imagined Paradise to be. Here, there was laughter, encouragement, plenty to eat, clean clothes to wear, and love. Elmer listened to stories about his father and for the first time in his life, wished he had known him. He met his Uncle Bill — a deaf mute just like his sister — and they would sit for hours engaged in a silent conversation of signs. Elmer helped his grandfather in the garden and learned how to cut down trees, to build and repair sheds, to tend chickens, to fix the roof, not to mention dozens of other skills which would serve him well in the years to come. He became adept at swimming in the cold mountain streams, and when he had shown that he was quite able to look out for himself, Elmer and his dog would go off into the woods and camp for several days at a time.

Elmer and his grandparents went to church every Sunday morning, and on Sunday and Wednesday nights. They attended church whenever it was open. The long sermons in the hot summertime were endurable when there was lunch on the grounds afterwards. The church lawn parties on Saturdays gave Elmer the chance to romp and play with other children and to become a part of this rugged and caring community. Elmer almost forgot city life. Occasionally he would remember the forbidden Bible and rejoice that he now had his own and was quite familiar with the promises in it. His grandparents told him how his father had loved the church and been faithful to it until he had married.

When Elmer turned nineteen, he found a job in a nearby timber camp. The work was hard, but he felt important and he could be counted on to always give a good day's work. Sometimes his assignment was in the mill where he helped saw poplar, chestnut and oak logs into lumber. At other times he went into the mountainous terrain to help load the wood onto train cars. Most of the loggers were older, and they were immediately impressed with E.E. Crawford's son. His quiet and unassuming manner, his willingness and ability to stay with the task at hand, and his obvious respect for his seniors, endeared him to these men of the woods.

The death of Elmer's grandmother made it necessary for his grandfather to move in with a brother, but not until contacts could be made on the grandson's behalf. His Uncle Mabry, who lived in Lynchburg, thought there might be job possibilities there. The men at the mill made up a gift of money, to help pay Elmer's rent.

Passengers on the bus to Lynchburg paid little attention to the handsome young man who stood six feet tall and carried the same shabby bag that he had used ten years previously. With little effort, his strong arms hoisted it onto the storage rack and he took a seat by the window. For a moment, his dark eyes filled with tears, but as quickly as they had come they disappeared. Elmer dropped his head, sighed and ran trembling fingers through his black, wavy hair.

He went directly to the YMCA, where he paid for a week's room and board. Elmer was pleased to learn that the fee included the use of the pool and gym. Next, he phoned his uncle who operated a store on the outskirts of the city and learned that an appointment was already set up for a job interview at the local shoe factory. Uncle Mabry volunteered to drive down to the Y on Sunday morning to take Elmer to church.

That service sealed Elmer's fate. It was here that he spotted Ida Faye and was immediately smitten. She was sitting across the aisle, a real beauty, the kind of woman who would stand out in any crowd. He had a difficult time listening to the sermon. The young lady's shoulder-length brown hair curled around an exquisite face, framed by a saucy navy blue hat. She wore a navy skirt and a white middy blouse with a sailor collar. Elmer's head pounded when she smiled at him and nodded.

On the way to Uncle Mabry's house for lunch, Elmer discovered that Ida Faye had only recently moved to town, and that she worked in a dry goods store. He began to plan what he might buy at that store.

Almonds Dry Goods Store was closed when Elmer finished his work at the factory, so he had to wait until Saturday to make a purchase. He decided that it would seem quite natural for a new boarder to need some towels, and so he approached the counter where Ida Faye stood. Her "May I help you?" sounded like an invitation from heaven, and, in spite of himself, Elmer stammered. Sensing his discomfort, Ida Faye quietly put him at ease with lighthearted conversation. In a very short time they were chatting about the services of the previous Sunday. She told him that she boarded with a cousin and gave him her address. Amazingly enough, before Elmer left the store, he had set up a date for the next church social. Somehow, looking back, it seemed that he must have floated back to the Y. Elmer was in love!

Christmas

El stood outside his great-grandmother's apartment, thankful that there was a wreath on the door. When his mother had reminded him that Ida Faye could be quite moody at Christmas, he instantly retorted, "Tell me about her moods!" Of late, Lady had begun to rub him the wrong way. He figured it was because they were spending so much time together. Whatever the reason, some of the shine of her pedestal was beginning to wear off. He took a deep breath and pushed the bell three times, hoping she'd hear at least one of the rings. The door opened almost immediately to reveal a smiling woman whose fingers looked as if they'd been frosted for dessert.

"Come on in while I wash my hands," she invited. "I've been making mints for the last two hours, and these old bones are looking for an excuse to quit."

As Ida Faye disappeared into the tiny kitchen El took a look around. The dining room table was covered with boxes and tins, and Christmas mints were spread on waxed paper — yellow stars, red Santas, green stockings and multi-colored ornaments — all fresh from the candy molds nearby. Dozens of Christmas cards greeted him from the slats in the wide venetian blind. El could barely see the sofa through the pile of wrapped gifts just waiting to be delivered. Every other available space — tables, desk, television, and stereo — was filled with holiday decorations.

The plant stand in front of the window glowed with the blooms from Ida Faye's collection of African violets, and a bright red cyclamen had been added to the top shelf. A beautiful poinsettia, draped in green tissue, showed a Christmas gift card through its thick foliage. El guessed that the large oranges in the red fruit bowl on the table were the annual offering from a relative in Florida. El uttered a silent *Thank you to God!* for Lady's fine spirits and smiled as she came back into the room.

"Man, this looks like Santa's workshop!" El enthused as he walked into the apartment.

"My neighbors think I'm crazy," Ida Faye grinned. "They say it's too much trouble to pull out all that stuff, but I tell 'em that every last thing they see is special. When I look at it I think about how I made this or that, or how my grandchildren made it, or about who gave it to me. Shoot, that's half my Christmas right there."

Her voice rose with excitement. "I decided this year that I'd see if I could still make good mints. I'm giving 'em to lots of people in this place who're just sitting around waiting to die. Not me! If I should go tomorrow I'll betcha they'll remember that I celebrated Christmas. I've got the biggest door wreath of anybody on the sixth floor," she said proudly, "even though some of these characters around here probably think I'm begging for presents." She laughed, "The sign that Annie made with the wreath says, 'SANTA PLEASE STOP HERE.' Most of these folks quit believing in Christmas a long time ago!

"I sat here last night, plugged my headset into the TV so I could enjoy the Christmas music, and just looked around and remembered," she paused. "Why, that blue madonna over there — I made it! Didn't have no arthritis then. I made some real pretty things in that ceramics class.

El watched as a wound-up Ida Faye moved to the side of the room and pointed to a frame. "I made this jewelry Christmas tree, too. Took a few things out of my memory box for it!" She pointed to a shiny medal, "This here was your great-granddaddy's scoutmaster pin. And you see that?" El peered at the piece his grandmother touched. "That's my Eastern Star ring. I wore it to every last one of the meetings! Course I never did much work with them, just sorta went to see all the people." Ida Faye stared off into the distance, "I believe that's why I had to trace my ancestors back to the waugh, to get into that auxillary." El grinned. He always got a kick out of how Ida Faye said war, and how she never seemed to know which "waugh" she was talking about. "Nope, I'm wrong," she apologized, "That was the D A R!"

Next, Lady picked out a sparkling treasure. "Your grandmama Jane gave me these rhinestone earrings one birthday," she said. "And look at this little fork; it's really a lapel pin and it's in my silver pattern – Chantilly. Course, Elmer and I just had cheap stuff 'til our twenty-fifth wedding anniversary," she confided. "My two girls were gonna give a big party for us, and they insisted that we had to have some nice tableware. So, I went down to the jewelry store and picked this out. Your crazy great-aunt said we'd answer every phone call that came in before the party with the word 'CHANTILLY' so people wouldn't forget."

Obviously tired of the jewelry tree, Ida Faye picked up a small, crude, rag doll, dressed in traditional peasant attire. "I put a red ribbon around this here Japanese doll a long time ago. I know the poor man who owned it would have been surprised to know that it ended up in this country."

"Where did you get this, Lady?" El asked as he fingered the rough fabric.

"Well, my sister's ex-husband took it off a dead Jap soldier on some island when the war was over."

El interrupted, "You call them Japanese, Lady!"

"You call them what you want. I was alive then and you won't!" she snapped. "Do you care to hear the rest of the story?" El nodded. "It was Copley who took it off the soldier. He was in service but it won't the regular soldier kind. They had to go in and build things for the army and then when it was over, they had to go clean up."

"Could he have been a member of the Seabees?" El suggested.

Ida Faye ignored the question and turned the subject back to the islands. "They always reminded me of my pajamas."

"Iwo Jima?"

His great-grandmother harumphed and acted like he had taken the words out of her mouth. El let her have the credit.

"Anyway," she continued, "Copley told me how these dead Japs were laying all over the place and he saw something around them's neck, and it was this doll."

"And he took it off!" exclaimed El. "That's gross!"

If Ida Faye heard him, she didn't let on. She just switched gears and moved to another part of the apartment.

"I guess you're not old enough to remember much about your Aunt Patricia?" Ida Faye quizzed as she moved toward the window. She touched one of the yarn "snow people" hanging from the plant stand. "Patricia was in between husbands one Christmas and didn't have much money. So, she and the children made all of their gifts.

"I'll never forget the Christmas before she died. Patricia was so sick from her cancer that she couldn't go out and buy anything. Instead, she gave all of us little promises of things she was going to make. Mine said that I was going to get a tablecloth. We kidded her about the notes, telling her that she'd just have to get well so she could do all that sewing. Everybody knew that she won't gonna make it," Ida Faye's voice mellowed, "and she knew it too. Sure enough, she was gone in six weeks."

Once again, Ida Faye quickly changed the subject. She invited El to look in the bathroom. "You'll see something sassy," she teased.

El stuck his head in the door and saw only a wreath taped over the tub and a little elf on the mirror. Confused, he commented, "They look OK to me."

"Aw, just shut the door and use the bathroom," commanded Ida Faye. "Then you'll know what I'm talking about!"

El did as he was told and laughed when he looked down at the toilet seat. A bright red felt Santa Claus smiled up at him, and when he lifted the lid, Santa covered his eyes. "I see what you mean!" he called out to Ida Faye.

"Yep, my neighbor in Portsmouth showed me how to make 'em. I gave one to most everybody I knew, but people got too sanctimonious to use them so mine may be the only one left. Don't bother me 'tall that Santa has his hands over his eyes so he can't see you pee," she chortled.

Ida Faye was standing at the bedroom door when El returned. "You see that little stuffed horse I've sat on my bed along side of Donald Duck and the monkey? I made that when I was visiting Annie about five years ago. She was putting together crafts for her church bazaar. Shoot, I caught on in a hurry, and before I knew it, she had me making them for her. I think Horse'd rather be with the other two than shut up in a box for another year." She wagged her finger at the animals. "I always tell them to behave when I leave them alone. I hope I'm not making a mistake — you know what they say, 'Two's company, three's a crowd.' We'll just have to wait and see," she winked.

El smiled as he remembered his earlier worries about Lady's mood. He helped himself to some mints as they passed the table, but declined the offer of a cup of tea.

Ida continued, "I don't have a Christmas tree unless you count the family tree." She pointed to the geneaology chart over the desk. "I can look at that and think about how it was when I was a child. We didn't decorate trees then, least I can't remember one 'til I was about fourteen. We just hung up stockings in Mama and Papa's room before we went to bed on Christmas Eve. I recollect one time we all slipped down the steps at 3 a.m. and Papa yelled out, 'Con sarn it, you young'uns, get back to bed!' You better believe we did, too!

"It was never a surprise what was in the stockings — a Roman candle, some sparklers, a squib, a pack of dried raisins, an orange, and a special treat. You kids today would turn up your nose at that. Back then it was different. It won't so much what was in the stocking, it was the fun of hanging them up and trying to go to sleep before Santa Claus got there. Then we'd rush out of cold bedrooms, yell 'Christmas gift!' and warm ourselves by the stove." Misty eyed, Ida Faye elaborated, "It was all that good food and the way everybody seemed so happy.

"We would have oyster stew for breakfast - that was a tradition in our community. The whole month of December, Papa would take oyster orders in the store. On Christmas morning, the men lined up in their buggies waiting for Number 1 to come rolling in at 8:30. All the women would be at their cookstoves, heating up the milk and butter. I remember one time the train was late and Papa said he won't gonna miss his Christmas oysters, so we had to wait 'til 10:30 to eat."

"Why did you call the train Number 1?" asked El.

"That was the morning train," replied Ida. "Number 2 came in at 5:15 p.m."

Without batting an eyelash, she picked up the story. "I didn't mind helping Mama make all kinds of cakes and pies because I knew we could eat everything we wanted at Christmas. There was chocolate pies, lemon pies, apple pies, sweet potato pies, chocolate cake, and a fresh coconut cake. Mama had her faults, but for Christmas, she was different.

"Come to think of it, she was like that at Easter, too. For the whole month before, we kids could watch where the hens laid and if we got to their nests first, we could have all the eggs. Then, on the day before Easter we got to dye the ones we had claimed. Otis would try to steal ours. And, on Sunday morning, Mama would serve us as many as we wanted fixed any kind of way we asked. Those devilish brothers of mine would ask for one to be scrambled, one to be fried, one to be boiled, and one to be poached. Mama would do it, just like it won't no trouble at all!

"But getting back to Christmas," Ida Faye took a deep breath, "since Papa owned the store, our Christmas shopping won't no problem. We'd just go down and pick out what we wanted. Papa chewed tobacco, and all six of us would give him a plug. We gave Mama celluloid hairpins. They were three for a nickle, and I remember that one of them was blue. She never seemed to mind getting six boxes.

"Mama made blackberry wine and she would bring it out at Christmas and let each of the kids have one glass. I remember sneaking a little extra and going out on the front porch where I couldn't stop laughing. Mama quit her winemaking soon after that, when she saw that Royal and Otis was getting too fond of it for their own good.

"We always shot off our firecrackers on Christmas afternoon. See this scar in my palm?" Ida Faye held out her hand. "That happened when I was firing one of my Roman candles. It went backwards and into my hand. I was just about seven years old, but I can remember Mama keeping my hand greased, and sitting by my bed all night. I nearly cried my eyes out it hurt so bad. A blister came up as big as a goose egg. That was the last firecracker I ever lit."

El examined the faded scar. "We always do that for New Year's," he said. "But, I guess you all didn't celebrate that like we do today."

"Nope, we young-uns didn't do much of anything like what you do today, but we still had fun. For instance, when I was fifteen, Mama and Papa let me go to a New Year's party at the Butler's house. Oh, it was some party! We went there every year, because they had a clock that told you the date. The big event for the evening was to watch it change over to the new year at midnight. That was the night I fell in love with John," a soft smile lit Ida's face, "when we played Post Office and he gave me a Special Delivery!"

El's eyes opened wide, "Wow, I'm all ears. When you gonna tell me that story?" he quizzed, leaning toward Ida Faye.

"Well," she hesitated, "not now, son. I'm plumb talked out for today. Besides, I believe I have something in that old cigar box that you'll want to see when we talk about John.

"Well, I have surely talked my neck off," she glanced at the clock on the wall. "I'd better give you these presents to deliver." She pushed some packages into his arms, "Take them to your grandmama Jane's and put them under the tree — and don't look at or squeeze a single one! I'll be there earlier than you on Christmas morning 'cause Jane is going to make oyster stew for me before the rest of the crowd shows up. It'll be good, I guess, but somehow it won't be quite the same, 'cause the oysters won't come in on Number 1." She winked at the overloaded boy and rushed him out the door.

El

———

There's only two things I want to do, El thought as he showered. His mother's yell brought the young boy back to matters at hand.

"Come out of there, El. You're gonna use up all the hot water again!"

El didn't rush as he picked up the shampoo. He knew the water would last; they'd finally bought a larger heater. Rushing bothered him. Pouring the last few drops into his hand, he made a mental note to keep the next bottle in his room so his sister couldn't leave him another empty one. The sleep cleared from his head as he stood under the stream of water and tried to think of how he could tell her in Spanish to stop using it all up. The only command he could think of was *Abra la ventana!* As he turned off the water he smiled as he caught the end of his mother's tirade, "... gonna miss the bus again and I'm not taking you!" He knew she would.

As El pulled the rough towel across his back he frowned as he remembered that this was the day he was supposed to carry Lady to the doctor. *Damn, I'm getting tired of this. It's something new almost every day now. Yesterday, it was the groceries, and then she couldn't be satisfied with that. She just had to go by the bank, and for what? To deposit a ten dollar check.* El let the scene play through in his mind. "That just burnt me up," Ida had said. "Nancy asked me to go to lunch. Then when we got there she said she was a little short of cash, so would I pay the bill. She wrote me this check and said it would be good today, so I gotta get my money while it's still there! I don't trust her too much."

Trust? She doesn't trust anyone. She'll ask me to read her mail to her, and then she'll pull out that magnifying glass and look at it herself. When we put gas in the car she's always gotta personally ask the price, as if I might be trying to cheat her. I'm beginning to think I made a mistake when I agreed to cart her around in trade for Bassy. Of course, I am getting some good stories for my writing class, but I don't know about the sacrifices I'm making.

El spoke softly out loud, "A bargain's a bargain, and I guess I can stand it for awhile longer. After all, college is just six months away." He tried to put Ida Faye out of his mind by running through the tricky parts of his solo for the upcoming concert.

Della's announcement that she was leaving in fifteen minutes cut short the singing, and he hurriedly dressed and grabbed a doughnut as he rushed out the door, hoping he had everything he needed for the day. The feel of the car keys in his pocket reassured him that he would be driving the Chevrolet later. *Maybe I'll get up the nerve to drive it to school soon. Maybe, just maybe, I can do something other than sing or read a story I've written and not be embarrassed.* His thoughts shifted gear... *I'm not embarrassed when I'm with Jenny. She makes me feel so comfortable. I can just be myself with her. I'm going to miss seeing her at school today. I'll have to find time between classes to call her and check on her sore throat. She's gotta get better for our duet.*

The bell was sounding as El climbed the school steps. As he rushed down the hall, several students waved and smiled; he responded with a shy nod. Two girls were waiting at his locker, purportedly to remind him of Spanish Club meeting after school. He was secretly pleased when one of the young ladies, Marie, asked him to autograph her year book, but tried to be casual as he signed his name under his picture. He blushed as he read the caption, *Handsome and talented, sure to succeed.* He promised to be at the meeting, knowing that he'd have to dash out in order to get to Lady's on time.

English class was first, and El grinned when he saw the "A" on his story about Lady's Christmas. Mrs. Bragassa asked him to read the paper to the class; El was thankful that she didn't insist on his coming to the front to do so. "What's that old lady doing now?" asked Bob from the back of the room. "Give us the latest of her wild adventures, El."

El nodded, then turned to meet the expectant gazes of his classmates. "Well, before I do, I want you all to promise that you won't tell. If Lady knew I was writing this about her and letting others hear it, she'd 'skin me alive,' as she would say. Not only that, but she'd really be mad because of the parts that I've made up."

Bob seized the opportunity to bargain. "How about this, El? You drive Bassy to school and we'll keep quiet." The loud chorus of 'All right,' 'yeah,' and 'that sounds good to me' sealed the agreement. El's 'Okay' didn't tie him down to a permanent date.

At lunch, El called Jenny from the pay phone near the cafeteria. As he hung up the phone, he saw Julie waiting for him. She obviously hadn't heard that El and Jenny were going steady. El grabbed a tray and stepped into the place Julie was saving for him. It was hard knowing what to say to the attractive girl. She had developed a crush on him after they attended the prom together — at her invitation — and El couldn't figure out how to change the relationship to friends-only status.

When he had told Ida Faye about the invitation she was visibly shocked. "You mean the girl asked you?" she exclaimed. "Why I never heard of such a thing. When I was a girl the boys asked us, and even if I had been so brazen as to try it, Mama woulda had a fit." Lady was dumbfounded when El explained that this was the fourth prom he'd been to, all at the girls' invitations.

El explained, "Lady, this is the fourth prom I've attended. The girls ask me and, get this, they pay for dinner. All I have to do is provide transportation and flowers."

"Well, I never," Ida Faye shook her head in disbelief.

El took the Activity Bus home after Spanish Club, went directly to the car, and headed to Lady's apartment. Ida Faye was waiting for him at the door but barely heard his greeting. Once again, she was not wearing her hearing aid. El shouted as loud as he could, "Hello, Lady. Are you ready to go to the doctor?"

"Humph," was her reply. "I'm never ready to go see him. If it won't so much trouble for everybody else, I'd find another one. I wish he'd retire, he's certainly old enough. But he's gonna stay right in there, maybe just to make my life miserable. He charges every time he speaks to me and expects me to pay him right on the spot. He can't wait for Medicare money, gotta have it from me." Her tirade ended, Ida Faye gave her great-grandson an appealing look, "By the way, El, I wish you'd drive me out to the hardware store when we finish. One of them flyers in the paper said they have a special on bathtub seats and I want to get me one. It's been a long time since I had a real bath in a tub — been scared I'd fall. Been taking those PTA baths so I don't stink."

El hesitated, then said softly, "I'm sorta in a hurry, Lady. I have an audition tonight for the senior play. Could we do it another day?" he asked.

Ida Faye's voice turned icy, "Just forget it, even though today is the last day they're on sale. I'll just do without it. I hate having to always ask other people to do things for me." She frowned as she picked up her purse and followed El out the door. "Believe me, it ain't all it's cracked up to be, this getting old. Everybody's got their own stuff to think about, and you just get the feeling that it would be good if you could go on and die, so you wouldn't be so much trouble."

El took a deep breath, counted to ten, and gave in, "Never mind, Lady, we'll go get the seat." Curiosity getting the best of him, he asked "What's a PTA bath, anyway?" The old woman gave a sly laugh and replied,

"You can figure it out for yourself, 'cause it means I wash the necessary parts, and the 'A' stands for 'ass'."

El blushed and immediately changed the subject. "Jenny and I are going steady," he began.

"You are!" exclaimed Lady. "Is she the one with the beautiful voice, the one who sang with you in church — the pretty girl?"

"Yep, that's the right one. I gave her my ring last week, and we were sitting in Bassy, too."

"Well, I never had a boy give me a ring in a car, but I can't say that for a horse and buggy." Ida Faye's eyes lit up as she buckled the seat belt and launched into another story, "John and I were at the Peaks, waiting for the sun to rise when he gave me mine," said Lady. "I remember it like it was yesterday. 'Twas a funny thing — Mama never did trust me much, but yet she let me take those trips with him. We'd get about three couples, in their own buggies, and we'd leave home about nine o'clock at night. It took us about five hours to get there. We'd tie up the horses at the hitching post and just sit there 'til about four o'clock, then up the rickety steps we'd climb and be standing on Sharp Top when the sun burst out over the mountains.

"It was on our second trip, and we was at the tying place when John told me he'd like to tie me up. I didn't know what he meant, but then he pulled out a ring. It won't no engagement ring or nothing, but he wanted me to wear it and let everybody know I was his girl. It looked so pretty to me, there in the moonlight, and it was all so romantic. I couldn't read the name on the ring 'til the sun came up, but it had my middle name, Faye, on it. I wore that ring 'til the day I moved to the city. Those were the days when Mama approved of John. One time she told me that since I'd gone with John to the Peaks three times, she guessed I'd marry him. I thought I would, too."

As they pulled into the parking lot at the doctor's office El made a mental note to get the full story about John. He helped Ida into the building and worked on math homework while she went back to be examined. A short while later, Lady came out and announced to anyone within hearing range that her blood pressure was 190 over 90. She added that the top figure didn't matter and the 90 was for her age and that Doc had said she was in the best shape of all his older patients. She paid for the visit without grumbling.

John

What can I tell and what can I leave out? Ida Faye thought. *I sure as shooting won't tell the whole story. El ain't no dummy. He's probably figured out it was pretty serious.*

When the doorbell rang, Ida Faye swallowed hard, and slowly moved to answer it. "Lordy, he's early," she muttered. "Don't give me no time to plan what I'll say. I gotta watch my words."

Ida had called El that morning to see if he could come by and take her to the bank. She wanted to put her rings in the deposit box so Jane wouldn't have another chance to tell her how unsafe they were in the apartment. During the conversation, El had pressed her, so she had promised that she would tell him about John when they got home.

"Hi, Lady," El grinned. "Let's hurry and get that bank errand done so I'll have plenty of time to get the real scoop on that John person. This may be my most important as-signment, yet."

"What do you mean, 'assignment'?" asked Ida Faye. "Who you planning to tell this to?"

"Aw, calm down," El soothed. "Don't get your blood pressure up. I have to do stories for my writing class. No-body but the teacher reads them and she doesn't know you. Besides, she's more interested in my style of writing and how many mistakes I make. If she gives it any thought at all, she probably figures I make 'em up," El lied.

"Don't you worry about my blood pressure, young man," Ida Faye retorted. "But, it just better be like you say. If I hear tell of you doing something different, that's the end of any deals we have ever made. Now, let's get to the bank so I can put these jewels away. Then we can come back here and have a little snack, and I'll tell you what you want to know." *Or, at least what I want you to know,* she mentally corrected.

At the bank, Ida Faye insisted that El position himself so he couldn't see inside the box, but could stand guard to keep anyone else from coming into the room. Ida was quick — the young man and the old lady were back in the apartment in less than an hour. El helped himself to some chips and opened cokes for both of them while Ida Faye settled herself on the sofa. She began a bit uneasily, "If you will look in the cigar box, you'll find a cameo pin. John gave that to me." She pointed to the box on the table, sighed and began, "Here's our story:

"I was fifteen and John was twenty. It was my first New Year's party. I knew that Marshall Butler was sweet on me. He always tried to sit by me at every church social, so I won't surprised when he invited me to the affair. Everybody knew about the Butler's New Year's parties; they always had a taffy pull and played Post Office.

"Course you kids today would think that was boring. Anyhow, it was a cold night and big logs were burning in the fireplace. The taffy come first. The girls went out to the kitchen to help get the syrup ready, and Mrs. Butler asked me to measure out the sugar and molasses. Then she put in the vinegar water and soda and set it on the big old wood stove. While it was cooking she told us girls we could go bring the boys out to the kitchen and help them get ready. Course, if you was going to pull taffy you had to have greasy hands. Lordy, we must have wasted five pounds of butter while we flirted with whichever boys we wanted to pull the taffy with." Lady's eyes looked past El and into another time... "Anyway, when the candy was ready and cooled and in a big ball, each couple broke off a long string, and then we had to pull on that 'til it got hard. We yelled and screamed and tried to see how far we could stretch it across the room."

I'll bet Lady was one big flirt, thought El.

"Since Marshall had asked me to the party, I went on and started pulling it with him. But then, when John sauntered over, I forgot all about being nice to Marshall. John grabbed a-hold of ours and old Marshall just walked away. John kept making all these wisecracks, and I laughed at everything he said.

"After that, we was washing our hands together and John reached over and squeezed my hand while it was wet. I blushed. Later, John was sitting by me in the parlor and here comes that Marshall — sat hisself down on my other side. Both of them tried to see who could pay me the most attention. Oh, I was treated so fine. They kept bringing me taffy and punch 'til I finally had to say I couldn't eat another bite or take another sip. Course I loved every bit of them making over me."

"You haven't changed a bit, Lady," El interrupted. "You still manage to have more men than women talk to you. And you probably were telling those guys some jokes, too, if I know you."

"Always did find men to be better company! Don't think I had to make up any jokes that night, though," came the quick reply. "Anyway, we started playing games. Only one I can remember was Post Office. John was "It" so he had to go out into the hall. Then Roger, who was the postman, announced a 'special delivery for Ida Faye.' Well, I went out to the hall just like I was supposed to, and John grabbed me and kissed me hard. I mean real hard.

"That was it for me. I was in love. I couldn't take my eyes off John. At midnight we all watched the big clock change its date to January 1, 1916, and before I knew it, John had pushed me over to where the mistletoe was hanging and was kissing me again. When Papa showed up in the buggy to take me home, John whispered that he'd see me soon. I don't even remember the ride home that night."

"So, how did he get around to asking you for a date?" asked El.

"He came over to the store three mornings later. I was in my room when I saw him tying his horse to the hitching post, so I made some excuse about needing to go down to the store. When I went in I could hear the men teasing him. The word had gotten around in a hurry.

"Right in the middle of the store was a big pot-bellied stove and Joe Stiff was sitting in his usual place in front of it. Course Papa was there and a couple of the regular fellows was sitting on the bench. They always liked to congregate at the store. Mama said they gossiped worse than the women. Old black Al was standing behind the stove, leaning against the counter. Course we called him colored then, but your grandmother Jane has got me out of that habit. If I say colored she'll always ask me real smart like, 'And what color might that be?' like hot butter won't melt in her mouth." Ida's look of disgust evaporated as she returned to 1916, "Anyway, John was leaning up against the pole under the Postum coffee sign.

"I moved up to where the yard goods was stacked. When the men saw me, one of them said something like, 'Here's the beauty now!' and I blushed and they all laughed. Papa told me to find out what John wanted to spend his money on, if he had any. While I was filling his can with lamp oil, John asked me if he could come calling on Friday night. I told him I'd have to ask Mama, but I knew it was gonna be OK. Mama had liked him, sight unseen, as soon as she heard he was coming down from Roanoke to help out his Aunt Ellie. You see, his Uncle Rake had fallen off the horse and broke his leg, so Ellie couldn't do all the work by herself. And John was the answer to their prayers!"

Ida Faye took a sip of coke, then continued, "Well, I was on the money. Mama said that I could date John, and everybody in the family took a shine to him right away. Shoot, they treated him like he was one of us. Many a Saturday night he was there when Mama fixed us up a supper of hot biscuits with lots of rich butter and homemade ice cream for dessert."

El made a face and Ida Faye swatted at him, "That was as good to us as pizza is to you kids, today," she admonished.

"John would always help the boys bring the ice up the hill to the kitchen. Matter of fact, he helped 'em get the ice off the pond once or twice and they brought it to the ice house in his wagon! Sometimes we'd have hoecakes instead of biscuits, and then we'd get to eat in Mama and Papa's room. Mama would put the big iron skillet on the stove in there, and we'd just stand around and wait for her to fry the next one. We young-uns used to fight to lick the ice cream dasher, but the first time John was there Mama let him have it and he gave me a lick. The boys teased me something awful.

"John fit right in, just like a member of the family. We'd sing hymns while Mama played the old pump organ. John sang tenor, and when we did 'In the Garden' I used to get tears in my eyes just listening to him. I don't like to hear that one anymore, though. It makes me sad. They sang it at Papa's funeral on October 12, 1928 and again at Mama's on October 12, 1936."

"Hold on just a minute," said El, "so I can make some notes." He hopped up and grabbed some paper and a pen from the desk. "Gosh, they both died on the same month and day. You say that hymn was called 'In the Garden'? Never heard that one."

"And you ain't likely to, either." Ida Faye snapped. "The hymn books today are too uppity to have the good old songs in them — that's one reason I stopped singing in church a long time ago."

"Now, Lady," El chided, "I've heard you do a little humming when I've sat next to you in service. But go on and tell me about John. If your family liked him so much, why didn't they want you to marry him?"

"They liked him, for awhile. Goodness knows, he was around most of the time. He'd come over when me and the boys went ice skating on the pond. Winters were colder then. Course we didn't have any skates, we just slid around on our feet. John would put his arm around me and we'd skate round and round. When there was a full moon, it was really romantic. We'd make a big fire on the bank. I remember one time Otis burnt his coattail trying to get dry. Papa had told him he couldn't go to the pond because of what he had done to the car, but Otis slipped off anyway. The burnt coat was a dead give-away. Mama wore him out."

"What had Otis done?" El quizzed.

"Well, we had just bought that new Model T Ford. Remember I told you we had the first one in the county, and Papa was awfully proud. He called a family meeting to tell us that he had paid $440 cash for it and it had two speeds, forward and backward. I remember we laughed when Papa said that the salesman had told him he could choose any color he wanted, so long as it was black.

"Otis was always wanting to fix things, and he was pretty good at it, too. Well, he got hold of the keys, drove the car into the barn and pulled it up on some kind of contraption he'd made. Then he tried to take the whole thing apart so he could see how it worked. I thought Papa was gonna have a heart attack when he found Otis in the barn with car parts laying every which way and him trying to get the thing back together. Papa had to have a man from Bedford City come over to do it." Ida Faye and El laughed together as they pictured the scene, but stopped abruptly when she added, "It's funny now, but won't nothing funny 'bout the beating he got with the buggy whip."

Ida Faye's eyes sparkled as she picked up on her story. Her anxiety had subsided and she was enjoying the telling. "John and me went to church socials and young people's meetings and to dances at the Odd Fellows Hall. Everybody expected us to get married. I stopped going with anybody else, until we had a fight. Then, just for devil, I'd agree to date Marshall Butler.

"I remember one time John slipped over to the house and saw Marshall's buggy. He didn't do a thing but put the front wheels on the back and hitch up the horse at the wrong end. Marshall was one mad fellow when he came out. After he got it so he could drive, John crept up from behind the porch and we both rolled on the ground, we laughed so hard. When we sat up, we won't laughing. John began to kiss me, and he told me he loved me and begged me to meet him secretly. I said I would.

"Soon after that, Mama changed. It won't too long before she told me flat out that I had to stop seeing John. I sassed her and said I was going to marry him. It was then that she told me if I did I could never come back home again. So just before Thanksgiving, John joined the army and went to Texas. Our love affair was over."

———

Ida Faye leaned against the closed door after El left. Slowly she made her way to the rocking chair and groaned aloud as she sat down. The pain in her joints was intense. Leaning her head back against the soft cushion, she closed her eyes and began to rock.

"Ida Faye?" It was John's voice. "I'll race you to the elm tree."

They were astride those beautiful beasts, the sun was warm on her face and there was a soft breeze. Without answering him, she tightened the reins and gave the command, "Giddiap." Beauty immediately began to gallop down the road, carrying her rider as if the two of them were one. Ida Faye's skirt flapped wildly, exposing most of her legs. *I don't care*, she thought, *It was Mama who made me have a side saddle and if I worry about my skirt, I'll never do more than a canter .*

She could hear John close behind her as she dug her heels into Beauty's side. Oh, how she loved to ride with him like this. She could almost forget her guilty feelings. John loved her, she loved him and they were safe for a couple of hours. The wooded area around the church yard would protect them from inquisitive eyes.

They walked the horses to the familiar posts. Ida Faye slid off Beauty into John's arms. Without speaking they tied up the animals and headed for the path. A few steps into the woods brought the privacy they sought. As John kissed her lips, her cheeks, her hair, her neck, her eyelids, she moaned his name. His hands slid to her breasts and once again she did not offer resistance. She opened her mouth to his kisses as they sank to the ground.

—◦—

The distant sound of the telephone broke the spell. Ignoring the persistent caller, Ida Faye closed her eyes, trying to return to the ecstacy of long ago. It was useless. She could only remember the pain and shame of discovery, the brutal buggy whip on her back as her mama yelled, "Slut," and the silence of her papa. She had seen John only one more time, when she and Elmer returned to the old home place to show off their new daughter, Jane. He had heard she was coming and was among the welcoming crowd. Gazing down at the tiny brown eyes he had whispered, "I didn't get your mama, so I'm gonna wait for you."

—

School Days

As El rang the doorbell, he reminded himself that it would be smart to be extra nice to Lady at this point. *Don't say anything upsetting,* he thought. *She just might be planning to give you a nice check for graduation.*

"Come on in, El," she called. Ida Faye was holding El's graduation announcement in one hand and her magnifying glass in the other. Moving both a few inches from her eyes, she enthused, "I'm mighty proud of what this says about you: 'Class of 1993, Honor Above All!' You are really something else! To think that you're honored above all them students graduating."

El laughed, "No, Lady, I've done right well but not that good. What you're looking at is the seal for our school. *Honor Above All* is the school's motto."

"Oh shucks," Ida Faye grinned. "I should'a known that. We had one too. Well, I hope I can come to watch you. I know it ain't the big thing today that it was when I graduated. Not many people finished school, then. Mama had Papa put up a huge sign in the store telling everybody that I was graduating from high school. Want to see my announcement? I used to keep it in the cigar box, but I took it out to add to my scrapbook."

Without waiting for a reply, Ida Faye reached in her pocket and pulled out a yellowed 3 x 5 card, handed it to El, and ordered, "Read it out loud." Grasping the chair arms, she carefully lowered herself into the nearby rocker to listen.

El politely lowered his head, as Ida Faye brushed tears from her cheeks, and looked at this new treasure from her memories. Engraved in a recessed rectangle on the front of a folded card was the date, 1920, and swirled across the numbers were the words, *Class of*. The year's original red color had faded to a muted pink. Carefully, El lifted this section, and mustering his best forensic voice, he read,

"The Senior Class of Montvale High School
requests your presence
at the Commencement Exercises
Monday Evening, May Twenty-fourth at eight o'clock
M. E. Church."

Turning the card he continued,

"Class Motto: One People! One Country! One Flag!
Class Flower: Red and white carnation."

"Man! I can imagine my class choosing a flower. Probably would be a stink weed!" He hesitated before he read the class names. "Aw, come on!" El stared open-mouthed at Ida, "Your class had only two people in it? And you still had a graduation?" She nodded. "For two people?" Ida nodded again. "You gotta be kidding," El grunted in disbelief.

"Nope, it's true," said Ida Faye, "me and Ollie Unstetler. More started out in high school but they quit. Some of the girls got married, and the boys was needed on the farms. It won't the same then as it is now. My brother Audie and I was the only two in our family to finish school, including Mama and Papa. The high school was fifteen miles from us, so they sent me up to Thaxton and let me board with an aunt so I could go. There won't no way I could have gone that far every day. When some of the younger ones come along, Mama moved up to Thaxton to an apartment, thinking she could stay there while two others finished, but living away got too hard and it cost too much so they had to give it up.

"Mama was set on us having an education." Ida Faye's eyes took on a far-away look, "She sent me to Roanoke to stay with a cousin for one year to go to seventh grade. The teacher we had back home was just out of high school, and Mama was sure nobody that young could manage us young-uns. She was probably right, too. I still have the book we used in my household science class. We did some cooking and learned about healthy foods." With obvious effort, the old lady pushed herself out of the rocking chair, "Hold on, I'll show it to you."

From a desk drawer, Ida Faye carefully removed a water-marked and ragged book and handed it to El. The faded pages were still attached to a leather binder, and two rusty clamps held it together. Turning the worn, wide pages gently, El noted that each one contained a recipe, enclosed in box fashion on the left side, while the right was filled with inked notes. El could see a remarkable resemblance to Ida Faye's penmanship in earlier years, before her eyesight worsened. He paused to read aloud:

"Of all beverages, water is the best, and very few people drink enough of it. About four pints should be taken daily to equalize the loss through the excretory organs. The two most common beverages served, tea and coffee, have no food value and if hot water could be used in place of these the nervous system would be greatly benefited. Tea and coffee are stimulants, and while they probably do no harm to grown people if taken in moderation, they are harmful to children."

"Now, that's a real gem," exclaimed El. "I don't like coffee or tea, but I think I'll pass on the hot water bit."

"Well, Mama used to drink what she called hot water tea. She'd add cream and sugar to a cup of hot water, so she must have known it was good for her," was Ida Faye's reply.

El was still holding the announcement and was anxious to hear about the special occasion, but he made himself wait for her to re-open the subject. In the back of his mind, El rationalized that it might be acceptable to mention 'graduation gifts' if his great-grandma kept talking about her own ceremony. She didn't disappoint him.

"Anyway," Ida took a deep breath, "they was all mighty proud of me on that graduation night. Me and Ollie sang a duet for the program — 'Whispering Hope' — and the superintendent gave a speech. The principal presented our diplomas and shook hands with us. It was a big occasion." She smiled, "I saw Mama wipe a tear away while we was singing. Then when we got home she served up ice cream and cake. She had me stand up in front of everybody and hold up my diploma and read it aloud. I don't think anybody knew that I left out the part that said I hadn't finished my Latin," Ida flashed El a wicked grin.

"I was sorta sad to be finished cause I knew I was gonna miss all the fun. We was always doin' some devilment. Once or twice I changed the grades on my report card. I learned to do that after I brought home a C in Algebra and Mama refused to sign it. I had to take it back to school and tell the principal that Mama said she won't putting her name on anything that had a C on it. It was embarrassing!"

Ida Faye switched gears, "I was scared to death of my Latin teacher. She could make me tremble just by calling my name to recite. She addressed me as Miss Doolin and I dreaded those days she'd send me to the blackboard. Ollie won't fond of her neither, so one day we just left after we ate lunch and got Jake to tell her we was sick and had to go home. Well, Mama got hold of that story and she wore me out with the buggy whip, even though I was 15 years old. Mama never was one to spare the rod. She thought it would cure anything."

El handed the graduation card back to Ida Faye. He restlessly shifted from foot to foot, but she kept talking.

"Mama just went to a few grades herself. Papa, though, went to the New London Academy. I found out a lot about that school when I was working on genealogy. It's been a school for two hundred years, and it was started by some rich people in the county. You know where I'm talking about, don't you?"

El acknowledged that he did, that he drove past it on the way to Smith Mountain Lake. "I didn't know that my great-great-grandfather had been one of its students," he said, "and I never really thought about it being that old."

"I don't know how Papa got to go there," Ida Faye continued, "cause his folks won't rich. Anyway, by the time he attended, it won't a private school anymore, like it had been. Thomas Jefferson knew about that school," she emphasized, "for it won't far from his summer home, Poplar Forest.

"Strange as it seems, the school almost had to close before the War Between the States because there won't much money. Then, somebody died and left everything to the school, so it was saved. It's just a regular school now, and one of our cousins was a principal there not too long ago," Ida Faye finished proudly.

El hadn't counted on hearing a history lesson, but far be it from him to try and stop Ida Faye when she was on a roll. He was glad to take a breather and go out to her car to retrieve one of her Papa's school books from the cigar box. A few minutes later, El was back with a small, weathered leather text in his hands. When he opened it at Ida Faye's bidding, El examined the loops and flourish of his ancestor's signature, "A. W. Doolin." His inspection revealed that *The Primrose: A Gift of Friendship* had been published in 1852, and each of its 128 pages was framed with a classic artistic figure. When Ida Faye asked him to read somthing aloud he chose some stanzas from a poem entitled "Lines Accompanying a Bouquet Given to a Young Friend!"

"Dear Friend — and yet,
Permit a little teaching,
That comes with Truth's beseeching;
Perhaps you'll call it preaching,
Still, don't forget.
This bunch of flowers,
That I for thee have braided,
With beauty's life pervaded,
Will all be withered, faded,
In a few hours."

Ida Faye interrupted El's reading, "That just shows how different my Papa and Mama were. Papa was the quiet kind, probably had a few poems in his head. Mama's stories about school won't like that. Her school just had one room with a big pot-bellied stove, and the boys had to bring in the wood. Them was some mean boys, too. They would hide the school bell at recess time and then run off to the woods. The teacher couldn't find the bell, and she couldn't find the boys, either!

"Mama said that one teacher used to make them recite all these sayings and one day they got tired of it. So they made a big sign with the teacher's name on it and stuck it on the iron fence by the school. Right beside it they put another one that said, *'Fools' names and fools' faces can always be found in public places.'* Course they was smart enough not to tell on each other, so the teacher never guessed who did it.

"Another time Mama told us about a family of bootleggers that lived in the community. Their daughter, Rubee, sat in front of Mama in school, and she said that the girl always had a little bottle of likker on a string around her neck and she would sneak nips of it all day. Mama said Rubee had bugs in her hair," Ida Faye shivered in pretend disgust.

"I guess I took after Mama, wanting to be sure that your grandmother Jane got a good education, too. We couldn't afford it — that's the truth — but I managed to come up with the money to send her to a little private school almost smack dab on the campus of Lynchburg College. El nodded; he had just toured that school as a possibility for future studies.

Ida Faye kept on with her story, "Miss Sally was teaching what they was calling 'pro-gressive education' and she just had about ten pupils. We thought Jane was naturally smart, and she sure learned a lot while she was there. But I can really get her goat when I tell about her tricycle story."

"You mean a trike, don't you Lady?" asked El.

"You call it what you want, I'll do the same," snapped Ida Faye. "Sometimes I would let her ride her *tricycle* to school. One day she didn't come home when she was supposed to. Jane was really late, now that I think about it."

El's thoughts wandered; he was losing interest fast. He realized, however, that if he expected recognition for his own graduation, he'd better not check out on stories about school. Just to let her know he was still listening, El exclaimed, "Several hours! Did you call the police?"

"Shucks, no," said Ida Faye. "In those days we won't afraid for the kids. The whole neighborhood looked after each other's families. It was safe. When Jane was just a little older, she walked about three miles to take piano lessons, by herself, went through a lot of woods, and I still didn't worry."

"You couldn't do that today," El commented. "You wouldn't dare!"

"And don't I know it," lamented Ida Faye. "Times have changed for the worse! That day, when Jane did come home I was waiting for her. I asked that young lady where she'd been, and she began the longest lie of her short life.

"She told how she left school as soon as the bell rang but her tricycle got stuck in the mud. She allowed that she pulled and pulled and pulled and pulled before she got it loose. Then she said she fell off it and scratched her knee. Next, she went back to the school to get Miss Sally to put Witch Hazel on the cut. Miss Sally used Witch Hazel for everything and it always cured," Ida Faye commented in a knowing voice. "Well, I won't surprised to hear Jane say that Miss Sally had left the school and gone to her house; that she took a long, long time to answer the door; that she couldn't find her keys to the school for a long, long time; that she couldn't get the door unlocked; couldn't find the medicine; and on and on and on."

El was laughing in spite of himself and thought how he was going to tease his grandmother about this one.

Ida Faye continued, "When Jane finished, she was so sure that she had told such a good story that I couldn't help but believe her."

"What'd you do?" asked El.

"Jerked her up and wore her out, that's what. I think I cured her on the spot. I felt sorry for her when she peed in school though," Ida Faye was onto another story and there was no stopping her.

"We was trying everything to bring in an extra dollar," she said, "so we decided to rent our house out — we had two apartments in it, don't you know. Anyway, me and Elmer and the girls moved just outside the city limits and rented a small house. It had the prettiest hardwood floors; Jane loved to tap dance and I wouldn't let her dance on those floors. We didn't have a bathroom inside, so she would go to the outhouse to dance. We used to tell her she must be doing the *Outhouse Shuffle*.

"While we was living there, she was promoted to second grade. One day she came home really upset. It seemed that the teacher asked who would like to read a story to the class and Jane said she would, even though she knew she was dying to go to the bathroom. Jane was just getting into the story when she let loose and couldn't stop peeing. She was crying and peeing all the way to the door at the back of the room, and some of the boys was calling her a *piss pot*."

El's face reddened at Ida's crude language and in sympathy for his grandmother. "How embarrassing," he groaned. "She must have wanted to die."

"Well, almost, I guess," Ida Faye nodded. "She stayed in the bathroom, crying, and her teacher came in and helped her get her clothes dry on the radiator. Jane didn't leave there 'til the other children had gone home. I felt sorry for her."

El decided he would never mention this story to his grandmother Jane, about the same time that he determined to end the day's visit. He dug into his pocket for his car keys and leaned over to give Ida Faye a hug.

"One more story," the old lady begged. "I promise to make it short." Defeated, El sank back into the chair and prepared to listen.

A victorious Ida Faye said, "One time I actually dreamed all the questions I was going to have on a geometry test."

"Aw, come on, Lady," El frowned in disbelief.

"I did," she insisted. "I was worried about that test. I didn't understand the first thing about geometry and had just memorized everything. I dreamed that I had the test in my hand and I could see every problem. When I woke up in a sweat, I was scared not to believe it, so I wrote them all down. The next morning I used my book and worked all of the problems and then went to school. Would you believe that when the teacher laid that test on my desk it was exactly like the one I had dreamed. It was the only one I ever made 100 on, and I never could conjure up another test, even though I tried !"

El shook his head and tried to stand. A gnarled hand — surprisingly strong — confined him to the chair's recesses. The voice droned on. "I don't know whether school days are our best days or not, but I sure would love to put on those shoes one more time and be young and free of cares and aches and pains. That's where you are in your life and I envy you, El. Oh, I was 'bout to forget. I have a little piece of money for you. I won't gonna ask you to take me to buy your own present. I guess you can always use money. I love you, and your great-granddaddy Elmer would have been so proud of his namesake." She sniffed, swiped at a lone tear and pressed a bill into the palm of his hand.

El grinned with pleasure and relief. He looked down at the note and exclaimed, "Wow! I've never had a hundred dollars before!" Now was not the time to let Ida Faye know that the chauffeur service would be ending when college began.

Health Care

About with bronchitis had kept El from driving Ida Faye to get groceries on Monday; his phone call had been less than satisfactory, between a hacking cough and her repeated, "What's that?" Finally, he managed to make her understand that he had been to the doctor, was taking an antibiotic, and hoped to see her in a few days. She complained about the inconvenience, but said she could make out and then started to tell him what she always did for her children when they had the same ailment. El interrupted, "Not now, Lady, I don't feel like listening." She complied.

Three days later, El felt well enough to fulfill his obligations. He stopped to get gas at the usual corner station, and once again, Gus – the attendant – begged El to sell the car. "You don't want this old thing," teased El. "Why, it's got 150,000 miles on it."

Gus grinned, "We both know what shape it's in El, and I'd make you a fantastic offer." He ran his hands over the smooth body, "So, if you change your mind..."

"You'll be the first to know, if I do," laughed the young man, handing him a ten dollar bill.

Ida Faye was waiting on the front porch, obviously pleased with her success in hauling down a batch of newspapers using one of the basket carriers from the hallway. El mentally allotted time for a stop at the recycling bins.

She patted El's arm and asked him if he felt better. His "Not so hot!" got lost in the sound of the revving engine and she replied, "That's good. Now, let me tell you how to really cure bronchitis. Jane used to have it a lot when she was little and we didn't need no doctor. She almost had pneumonia one time, but the old remedy came through, and I was able to break it."

"Here we go," said El. The double meaning of the words went right past Ida Faye.

"I always was a pretty good nurse and knew all the old ways of healing. You didn't fill yourself with a bunch of dope back in those days. Won't no danger of anybody having a 'drug problem,' as they call it. Take for instance that time when Jane almost got pneumonia. She was coughing and had a temperature of 103 degrees. She was wheezing so, she could hardly get her breath. I didn't do a thing but put her to bed on the sofa — there won't no heat in the bedroom — and fixed up a mustard plaster.

"I sat right there beside her, kept washing off her face and arms so's the fever would come down, watching that the mustard plaster didn't burn her. Every once in awhile, when she was willing, I'd give her a little water to drink and sometimes, a bit of chicken noodle soup. I sat up with her all night, and at six o'clock the next morning, that thing broke. She was sweatin' up a storm, so I kept her covered up real good. Course I had to give her a little bit of whiskey to bring her back up from all that weakness. Otherwise, she woulda' died. When she woke from a long nap, she didn't have any more temperature, won't wheezing, and was hungry. It didn't take but a few days for her to get well."

An incredulous El remarked, "You mean you gave whiskey to a child?" Before she could answer, he continued, "What in the world is a mustard plaster?"

Ida refused to be rushed. "Well, about the whiskey — it was necessary, so it was just like any other medicine. Some people call the plasters 'poultices,' but they're all the same. You just spread mustard out of the jar onto a cloth, real thick, like it was a sandwich. Then you cover it with another cloth, so it won't ooze out. You take that and put it right on the sick person. Course you can use dry mustard instead, but you have to mix it with egg white. It don't take no time 'til the mustard starts burning, so you have to be careful. It works fast, too, — opens up all the pores and gets right to the heart of the congestion. Some people would rather make onion plasters, but I always thought mustard was the best. Now, if you think you aren't over that bronchitis, I'll fix you one and you'll be well in a hurry."

"Thanks, I think I'll just stick to my medicine, if it's all the same to you," El gave her a smile. "But I'd really like to hear about some of the other remedies you used," he continued, excitement edging his voice. "It would make for interesting writing! I've heard my grandmother Jane talk about how you used to dose her with castor oil, and how terrible it was."

"It won't no treat — and that's for sure!" snapped Ida Faye. "I used to say that I could tell when the girls needed a good dose, just the same as when they needed a spanking. It really cleaned them out."

"I'll bet it did!" commented El. "Wonder why they didn't perk it up like they do medicines now, so it wouldn't taste so bad?" he mused out loud.

"Oh, they tried," Ida went on. "Most people took it in a little orange juice. Course, it did a pretty good job of making you hate oranges. Did you ever hear the story about the time Jane and Charles went out selling candy?" asked Ida.

"Don't think so," El replied, marveling at her quick change of topic.

"Charles lived next door and was Jane's good friend. They was always trying to think up ways to make some money, 'cause Lord knows, we parents didn't have a dime to spare! Anyway, they would go up to Uncle Mabry's store and work a deal with him so's they could get twenty-four candy bars. He was so crazy about kids — didn't have any of his own — that they could wrap him around their little fingers. Then, they would go out from door to door and sell the candy for five cents a bar. When they had sold it all and paid Uncle Mabry, they ended up with twenty-five cents profit."

"Twenty-five cents profit!" exclaimed El. "They'd have to sell twenty-four bars to make twenty-five cents?"

"I knew that would make you perk up!" laughed Ida Faye. "I have a hundred stories about those Depression days, but let me finish about the candy. Jane and Charles divided it up into two boxes and went out on this hot summer day to sell the chocolate. The way they told it was they went to a few houses but nobody wanted to buy, so they decided to walk through the grounds of the college. They sat themselves down under a tree, and when they got up, they had eaten up all the candy."

El narrowly avoided hitting the truck which had made a sudden stop in front of him without any warning. "They ate twenty-four bars of candy?" El whistled under his breath. "What size were the bars? What kind of candy was it?" asked El.

Ida pursed her lips together in thought, "Same as they are today — Milky Way, Baby Ruth, Butterfinger, and my favorite, Mounds. As far as I can tell, they was about the same size," she replied. "Anyway, they came on home, with stomach-aches of course, and worried about how they would tell us. They knew they had to, 'cause they had to pay Uncle Mabry and they didn't have no money. Finally, they did 'fess up, so Charles's mother and I brought them out in front of our houses and told them they could choose their punishment. They could take either a switching or a dose of castor oil. Jane chose the switching, and I made her go break her own switch off the tree. I always did that, and she knew better than to bring a puny one. Charles chose the castor oil, and after that Jane decided that her friend Charles won't so bright."

As El pulled into the market parking lot, Ida Faye pulled her grocery list from her purse and put it in his hand. As usual, he couldn't decipher *all* of the scribbles, but he had gotten better. When he read the list aloud, Ida Faye would fill in the illegible items from memory. "What kind of soup is this?" he asked.

"I don't have no soup on the list," came the quick reply. "You must be talking 'bout soap — Octagon soap. I want to see if they still sell that. I've got so many stains on my clothes and I can't see them. So then Jane tells me that what I'm wearing needs washing. If I can find some Octagon, I can be sure that they're clean. Used to use it all the time and sometimes it was kinda like a medicine."

"Say what?" queried El.

"Well, sometimes I had to use it to wash out the girls' mouths, sorta like a disinfectant, you know. It worked right well, too. If they said a bad word, that's when I'd get out the ole Octagon and go to work on them."

Without thinking, El blurted out. "How about giving me an example — what did they do to deserve Octagon?" He instantly regretted opening his mouth when he noticed curious shoppers looking their way. Course, that didn't faze Ida Faye. She didn't have to think long.

"You mean like the time I caught Jane and Charles out in the shed? They won't no more than six or seven years old, but I knew something was going on, so I called Jane in the house and made her tell me what they was doin'." El groaned and tried to get Ida interested in picking out some bread. It was too late, she couldn't be stopped! El moved to distance himself from the old lady, but he wasn't too far away to hear, "Jane said that I probably wouldn't know the word but they called it *fucking*. Did I ever scrub her mouth out with Octagon!"

El quickly took Ida Faye's arm and steered her to another part of the store. She was in great form now! As they moved past the shelves, she commented on every product she had ever used for medicinal value. The nail polish brought to mind the time she had cured chigger bites by painting a line around her waist. The tea and coffee aisle triggered a lament that there was no sassafras tea, like her mother always gave to the kids for a spring tonic to tone up the blood. The Vicks salve reminded her of croup tents and steaming pans of water, and she wondered out loud what had become of the old standby, Cloverine Salve. Needless to say, shopping took much longer than usual.

Ida Faye stopped dead in her tracks at the meat freezer, looking it up and down. "Whatcha looking for, Lady?" El peered over her shoulder.

"I was just checking to see if they had any fat meat so I could show it to you. While I was thinking about all those things we used for medicine, I remembered the time when Annie was little. I found her out beside the house, sprawled on the ground, and coughing up a storm. There was a big piece of fat meat beside her. Royal always teased her a lot, and he had told her that she could turn herself into a boy if she would swallow a piece of fat meat while standing on her head. She was sure disappointed that it didn't work."

El made a face in disbelief and followed Ida Faye to the vegetables and fruits. When she saw the bananas, she asked El if he got enough potassium in his system. Then she was back into how they used to go downtown every Saturday and she'd put Jane in a movie while she shopped and payed bills. The movie just cost a dime and the ushers all knew Ida Faye, since she was there every week, so they would let her take Jane in, help her find a seat, and then come back to pick her up later.

Ida Faye kept on talking, stretching El's patience to the limit. "After the movie we would go down to Woolworths and have a banana split for ten cents. Sometimes the fountain would be so crowded we'd have to stand behind the people who were already eating, and sorta' look over their shoulders so they'd hurry up and give us a seat."

"How rude!" commented El. It didn't faze Ida Faye. As soon as they were en route to her apartment, she told him that colds wouldn't be so bad if you'd drink a lot of hot, syrupy-sweet lemonade and that you could stop hiccups by pressing your hand at the back of the neck and at the same time taking nine swallows, without breathing. El learned all sorts of trivia on that trip home: that his grandmother Jane had gone into convulsions when she was teething, where-upon Ida Faye had placed her in a warm mustard bath; that Annie had been given Ipecac when she was about to choke on phlegm; that salt water sniffed up the nostrils beat any nose drops; that Lady kept a bottle of Spirits of Amonia on hand for nervousness; and that a local girls' school was ru-mored to put saltpeter in its food so the girls wouldn't be so hot after boys. By the time El dropped Ida Faye off at her apartment, he had all the material he needed for his next writing assignment, and he was, as Ida Faye would say, "Plumb tuckered out!" from listening.

The Depression

*El could think of a thousand things he'd rather do than go to lunch with Ida Faye. She frequently hinted at it, after they had gotten the groceries, and even though he felt a bit guilty, he usually found an excuse. Today, however, he had agreed readily. It would save him the cost of a meal and at the same time provide new material for his writing class on "How Lady Faced the Depression."

His classmates had made all kinds of conjectures when the teacher had given El that assignment, but one in particular prompted the most laughter: "She was probably standing on top of a tall building and keeping a head count when the suddenly penniless men were hurling themselves to the street below!" exclaimed Bill. Remembering the guffaws that followed this comment, El smiled to himself as he pulled into the parking lot at MacDonald's. He helped Ida Faye get seated in the non-smoking section and put her cane where others wouldn't trip over it. He ordered his usual cheeseburger and fries and got a chicken sandwich and coffee for his great-grandmother.

El could hear Ida Faye talking before he actually got back to the table. "... Take that chicken, for instance. It was 'bout the only meat we could afford in those days, and there was a time when I thought I never wanted to see one again. Course, Mama and Papa had always raised chickens so I won't no stranger to them, but I never knew I was gonna have to learn to kill them and pick those feathers off! I got to the place that I would almost vomit at the smell of one cooking."

Damn, thought El. *I've obviously made a mistake and it's too late to recoup. She's gonna tell all the gory details while I try to eat. And everybody in the whole place can hear her. How gross!*

He was right, of course. Ida Faye continued, "I remember the first time I tried it. Mama had always wrung their necks off, but I decided to tie one up on the clothes line and cut off its head with a butcher knife. The knife won't sharp enough, and the poor old hen kept a-jumping and a-jerking. Me, I was sweating up a storm and yelling for Elmer. He had to finish off the job. After that, I went back to the old wringing method. Shoot, it didn't take no time to get that head off and see the old bird flop all over the ground. As soon as she got still, I'd douse her in scalding water and start picking off them feathers. Those pin feathers were the hardest."

El almost gagged on the hamburger in his mouth. Ida Faye didn't even pause.

"Makes me think of when Mama was gonna cook up a lot of chickens. She'd make the boys kill 'em. They'd bet on who could work the fastest. They'd line up, run to the chicken house and get a hen, tie up the feet, run back to the yard, wring the neck, put the bird in the water kettle and pick off the feathers. When they was finished they'd yell for Mama to come inspect. I'll never forget the time Otis got mixed up and dipped the live hen in the water before he wrung the head off. It was a-squawking like mad, and Otis dropped it and began to swear. Course Mama slapped him for cussin' and he could have killed us for laughing so hard while he was a-trying to hold that wet hen tight enough to get its head off. For days we teased him — said he looked madder than a wet hen — 'til Mama finally made us stop."

If El didn't know better, he would have believed that Ida Faye had magical powers that allowed her to talk without breathing between sentences. She plowed into the subject of his paper like a steam-roller flattening blacktops.

"Yeah, I remember those Depression days. They won't easy. Elmer was cut back to eight hours a week at the sign company, and my brothers didn't have no steady work so they was living with us. Royal did get himself a McCarthy's bakery route for awhile. Jane and Annie loved it when he came home at night and had some buns and cookies left over. Their favorite was always the cream puffs. Course, they didn't realize that every time he had something left, it meant he was losing money. He never let on though. That was one thing you could always say about him, he won't selfish and he loved those girls of mine. When Roosevelt came out with those CCC camps, Royal got himself into one."

El leaned towards Ida Faye, his flagging interest restored, and remarked, "That's the second time you've told me about somebody in our family being personally connected with the New Deal. We've just been studying about that in history, 'bout all the things FDR did. I never thought about being connected to it personally."

"Well, it was personal, all right," said Ida Faye. "The CCC boys was making parks and doing all this work out in the woods. They lived in barracks and wore the most handsome tan-colored uniforms. Royal looked right nice in his! The Civilian Conservation Corps kept many a young man from starving, and they had a roof over their heads, and decent clothes. I know we was grateful. Royal was probably eating better than we was in those days.

"Times were hard for everybody, and people were always trying to break into houses to steal. They sure enough tried ours," she persisted.

"Well, we never could figure it out, either — we didn't have nothing to steal. But, we had boarders and they sometimes had a little money. We always thought it was one of them that was trying to steal from each other. Elmer had a gun, and more than one time he'd wake up and hear somebody in the house. He'd get that gun and slip around to the girls' room, in the dark, and tell them not to be scared. Course, they always were," Ida Faye assured him.

"I would think so," said El. "Did he ever catch anybody?"

"No, he chased somebody down the alley one time, fired a shot at him, but the man got away. I can still see us, 'bout four o'clock one morning, standing on the front porch, Elmer with his gun, the police with blood hounds, and Jane and Annie in their long nightgowns. 'Twas like something you'd see in a movie!" Ida Faye concluded, her head lifted with pride.

"Wow!" said El. "I'm more impressed all the time with the things you tell about my great-granddaddy!"

"That man won't afraid of the devil!" exclaimed Ida Faye. "There was a prowler going around Lynchburg. He would sneak into peoples' houses after they had gone to sleep, and they'd wake up and find the man sitting at the foot of the bed. They said he didn't wear a shirt and that he greased his body so he could get away fast, but I don't know if that's true or not.

"Anyway, he didn't hurt anybody and he didn't steal. But one night a man named Lacy shot him dead. It won't long after that people told us that Elmer looked like that Lacy who'd done the killing. A couple of nights later something happened that made us believe it," said Ida Faye. She paused and El quickly intoned, "Well, what happened? You can't just leave me hanging!"

Ida Faye, pleased with his interest, picked up the story line, "I was in the Memorial Hospital, don't you know. I had just had my operation, and Elmer got Lewis to drive him over to see me. Well, they get on this dark street in a rough part of town, and wouldn't you know it, they give out of gas! So while Lewis waits in the car, Elmer takes a can and heads for a filling station. It won't long before he knew somebody was following him, and sure enough, three men jumped on him. Elmer, being the strong man he was and a Golden Glove boxer and all that, hit them pretty hard, enough to make them run away. He figured he came out lucky, because all he had was a broken finger. We always believed those varmints thought Elmer was that Lacy who killed the prowler."

"That's some story, Lady!" El enthused, mentally making notes to put in his next paper.

Happy that she had impressed El, Ida Faye energetically continued her saga of past hardships: "I guess we woulda never made it if it won't for Elmer's Uncle Mabry. He owned a store — remember, he's the one with the candy bars? — and every day or two he would slip by for a little visit and bring along a bag of groceries. Course, he would always say they was vegetables that won't fresh enough to sell or cans that was bent, but we knew that won't the case. We would charge the groceries we bought at the store, and we tried to pay a little bit each week, but we never got that bill paid up. I know that Uncle Mabry just sent us a note saying we didn't owe him anymore money, cause it was no way we had settled our debt." Ida Faye's eyes grew misty as she whispered, "He was one good man!"

Suddenly, she took a look at her surroundings, "Lord a' Mercy, El! Here we are, sitting in this restaurant eating good food and thinking nothing about it. Well, there won't no going out to eat during Depression days. Our family had many a meal that won't nothing but biscuits and gravy. I'm not talking 'bout that special sausage gravy that your dad makes on Saturday mornings, either. Ours was made from fat-back grease. And we had to thin the milk down with some water."

"Ugh, that sounds awful," El grimaced in disgust. "What exactly is fat-back?"

"It's the fat meat from pork, the same as I told you Annie tried to swallow so she could change to a boy," Ida Faye reminded him. "You'd fry it to get all of the grease out, add flour and salt and pepper, then you'd put in some water and some milk, and it would get thick. We called it 'thickening gravy,' and when it was poured over hot biscuits, it was good. I remember one time when Jane and some of her friends were playing Mother and Children right outside the kitchen door. Jane was the mother and she took a child to the doctor. When the doctor asked Jane what she had been feeding the young'un, she put her hands on her hips and shook her head. In a disgusted voice she said, 'Well, gravy, doctor. Gravy!' as if he ought to know.

"Course, I still have some good memories of those days. I used to take the girls over to the Appersons. They was the parents of my best friend, Bootie, and they had this big old house and a huge chicken coop. I think they had cows, too, but I can't be sure. Anyway, Bootie would take her two kids and we'd all spend the day together.

"The kids loved to go out to the chicken house and get the eggs. They waited around for the hens to lay. But the best part of the day was eating at Mother Apperson's table. She was a good cook and had vegetables from her own garden and plenty of milk. Now I do remember. They did have cows 'cause they had their own milk. Course it was raw, not pasteurized like today.

"Mother Apperson would cook up so much food, like cakes and pies, and put all of it out on the table at the same time. In those days the grown-ups got to eat first, and the kids had to wait 'til they was through."

"Unfair!" teased El.

"You young'uns today don't know how good you've got it," replied Ida Faye. "You wouldn't have lasted an hour back then." Her sharp words emphasized the fact that she meant what she said, but even her temper was forgotten as the great-grandmother continued her story.

"After we all stuffed ourselves, we'd clear off the dishes and then Mother Apperson would just leave the food on the table and cover it with a clean tablecloth. That way, we could go back and help ourselves whenever we felt like it."

"Weren't you afraid of food poisoning?" asked El.

"Humph!" came the reply. "I never heard of anybody having that."

"Could you afford to have ice during those days?" asked El.

"Sure, we had to have some to keep food from spoiling. The ice truck came down our street every day, and we would put up our sign if we wanted some. The kids used to love to run behind the truck and pick up pieces that fell on the street from where the ice was chipped. We usually bought twenty-five pounds at a time."

"Weird!" said El. "How did you pay for it? Did you have a job in those days, Lady?"

"Of course not. Women didn't work back then. It was their job to stay at home and take care of the family. I wouldn't have thought of such a thing. Now, I did bake some pies for Elmer to take to the factory to sell at lunch time. I would make lemon pies, and he would sell them for a nickel a slice. Course, we always hoped he wouldn't bring any back home 'cause we couldn't eat them. They used turpentine in the sign company, and the pies would get that taste in them."

"Lucky that someone didn't get poisoned," El interjected. "I don't believe I'd have made it back then without my Big Macs." He glanced at his watch, cleared the table and emptied the trash in a nearby container. Then, offering his hand to help the old lady, he said, "Ready to go?"

As Ida Faye struggled to get to her feet, she made an unprecedented reference to her bent shape, "You know why I can't straighten my back and stand up tall, don't you?" El dared not indicate that it might have something to do with her age, so he simply shook his head. "Well, it's because of the Depression."

El tried not to laugh. "Do what?"

"Well, when the doctor took all those X-rays and said my bones was thin and I had that osteo-something, he asked me how many operations I'd had. When I told him about the female one I had back in 1933, he wanted to know if I'd taken hormones. I told him that I carried around a prescription for something for a long time but never had any money to have it filled. He said that was too bad because it might have kept me from having all of this mess now. Lordy, if I'd a known that, I would have certainly gotten that medicine, one way or another."

On the trip back to Ida Faye's apartment, she continued to recite stories from the Depression. It was quite obvious — to quote her favorite phrases — that Ida Faye could "talk her neck off."

"I'll declare, El. One reason this car has been so special is 'cause we never had one during the Depression. Elmer had his wheel to ride, but the rest of us walked, or caught the streetcar."

"Elmer had a what?" asked El.

"A wheel," she looked at him as if he were slow. "You know, a bicycle. He rode it to the sign company every day. Shucks, sometimes he even came home at lunchtime on it. I'd see him turning the corner up the street, and I'd fly to the kitchen and get something out for him to eat. He didn't care what it was — beans suited him just fine — and he certainly won't gonna be no trouble to nobody. He was always looking out for the other fellow. Why, we never sat down to eat a meal that he didn't wait for everybody to fill up their plates before he'd take anything. I never let on that I noticed. I can tell you for a fact, though, if he was still here today, I'd fix his plate first.

"There won't no denying it, Elmer was one of the finest men that ever lived. When money got so scarce, he took a job at the church being a janitor. He won't too proud. His family meant more. On Sunday mornings in the winter, he'd leave the house at 4:30 a.m. and ride that wheel down to the church. He'd have to get the old coal furnace going so the building would be warm for us. Annie was too little to notice, but I know that job embarrassed Jane, especially when some of the big shots at church would ask Elmer to do something in front of people, like move a piece of furniture.

"I guess the hardest thing he ever had to do in the job was clean up a man's brains off the floor." El just about missed a stop sign on that one! "Mr. Green was a member of the church. He was there every time the church doors was opened, just about. Well, he lost everything he had in the crash and so he went down to the church one morning, went back to the furnace room, spread newspapers around, and blew his head off with a shot gun. Elmer found him when he went in to start the fire."

"God! How awful!" exclaimed El.

"It was pretty bad, but Elmer figured he didn't have no choice. Elmer was too kind for his own good. Fact of the matter was, that habit just about killed us. He signed on a note for a man at the factory, never dreaming that he was doing anything more than helping out, and the man couldn't pay the $250. Well we didn't have an extra fifty cents, much less two hundred and fifty dollars. We was desperate. I told Elmer I was gonna leave him for doing such a stupid thing, but I knew I won't going anywhere. Anyways, I didn't have one dime myself."

"What did you do?" asked El.

"We had to pay it. We let the mortgage installments go, but we still couldn't make ends meet. Finally, we did like everybody else — took bankruptcy. In those days that was the last straw. Won't like it is today when folks act like they think nothing of it, like it's due them. Back then it was a disgrace and you couldn't get no credit. I thought we'd never get back on our feet. You young'uns have everything handed to you on a silver platter, so I doubt you'd make it if something like that happened to you! I sure hope you don't ever have to find out."

"Sounds depressing — guess that's where the label, 'Depression' came from," mused El.

"Yeah," Ida Faye nodded, you can get to feeling mighty low when you don't have enough money. I remember Elmer used to bring some old clothes home from a bag that was at the factory. Every once in awhile there'd be something in it that would fit Jane, but she always hated to wear anything that came out of the 'rag bag,' as she called it. That's probably why your grandmother always looks so dressed up now.

She used to say that when she grew up she won't never gonna wear anybody else's clothes again. It was hard, I can't deny that, but we made it, and I'm proud to say that I don't owe anybody a dime! I even get letters from stores, wanting me to get a credit card. Just think, little ole Ida Faye Crawford now has people begging her to owe them money!"

El dropped Ida Faye and her groceries off at the apartment, then pretended to have an urgent errand to run for his mom, leaving her in mid-sentence. Hearing about the Depression had left him feeling sad and tired. El realized that he was indeed very tired. Tired of being nice, tired of Ida Faye's whims, tired of the whole deal — he had had enough! El wanted to wrap it up, write this final story for his class, keep his promise to drive Bassy to school, and get on with his own life. There was no indication that Ida Faye was fading in either strength or determination. She would probably live to be one hundred! But, it was time for somebody else to give her a hand. Now, all he had to do was to figure out how to tell his great-grandmother that his "shofering" days were over.

The Departure

The Departure

⌒⌒

*E*l pulled the last item from Ida Faye's cigar box. She had left a message on his answering machine, as usual ending it by saying her name, as if she were signing a letter. The vibrant voice asked that he take her to the Division of Motor Vehicles (she called it the "car place") so she could sign Bassy over to him. Hallelujah!

El was amazed at the timing. *I'm ready to quit! I need some time to just hang out.* He grinned in anticipation. *She's going to give me the car.* There's only one more story to be told, and, he gazed at the object in his hand, *this old newspaper clipping of some babe is it. How lucky can I be?*

El stared at the faded picture of what he supposed was a pretty young woman, if you happened to like that type. He could barely make out the words across the top — it seemed she was the winner of something in Lynchburg that had taken place in October of 1933.

El had never really been interested in watching those beauty pageants, but he was surprised to find out that Lynchburg had perhaps participated that long ago. Anxious to sew things up with Ida Faye, El arrived a few minutes before 9:00 a.m. and had to wait for her to finish dressing. He paced while she shouted to him from the bedroom, wishing that she would get on with it. Common sense convinced the teenager it would be best not to rile her. She could decide to keep Bassy after all.

As they drove towards the DMV, El asked Ida Faye about the beauty queen from the newspaper.

"Oh, they may have called her a beauty queen, but she won't that, although the girls was all attractive," she said. "It was really a contest to see who could get the most votes. They had ballots in the newspaper, and the one who got the most was queen of the Halloween parade. 'Miss Halloween X,' I believe they called her.

"Oh, that was a big event downtown on Halloween night. The queen and her court rode on an elaborate, decorated float. They was dressed in evening gowns and had bouquets of real flowers. And right behind them came the mayor and the city council. The parade had marching bands, and clowns, and all kinds of stuff, and then it all finished up with a fine ball at the old armory. We only went to one of them — rode the street car down — but it was mighty impressive.

"That was the year that my girls worked so hard trying to get up votes for the queen. They went around the neighborhood and begged for all the newspapers so they could vote. I think their girl won that year; she was a senior at E.C. Glass High School. Jane and Annie thought the whole ticket was lots of fun, but I guess you kids today would say it was boring."

El remained silent but admitted to himself that it did sound pretty dull. He wondered, on the other hand, how Halloween was celebrated when his Grandma Jane was young. "Did the kids play Trick-or-Treat then?" he asked Ida Faye.

"Nope, didn't even hear of it 'til sometime in the forties," was the reply. "Jane and Annie was grown by then. When they were young, children just dressed up in homemade costumes and went around the neighborhood doing things. All the kids would wait 'til it got dark before they went out. They did mischievous things, nothing mean. They'd ring doorbells, and before anyone could come to the door, they'd run away. Or they'd put leaves on porches or soap up windows.

"I remember one time a man on our street turned all his lights off, and when somebody got ready to ring his doorbell, he sicced his dog out the door. Did they ever scramble!" she laughed. "I heard that out in the country they used to turn over outhouses!"

El groaned but Ida Faye ignored him. "We had Halloween parties at the church, too. The building was five stories high, had big old rooms, and dark basements, and lots of stairs. We Sunday School teachers would decorate with 'haints' and goblins. The part the kids liked the best, though, was the ghost walk. We'd run a string all over the church, up and down, in and out, around the high places and all, and you just walked through, in the dark, holding onto the string. We'd have scary noises along the way."

"That does sound cool," admitted El.

"It was," Ida stated. "We ended up the party with refreshments like ginger cookies and cider. While they was eating, we'd tell ghost stories or you could have your fortune told. I used to do that. I got pretty good at reading a person's palm, even if I do say so myself."

"You believe in that stuff, Lady?" El quizzed.

"Well, I'll put it this way. I can't say I don't believe it. I could look at life lines and tell people all kinds of things about themselves, and lots of times they'd tell me it was true."

"Aw, come on. They knew who you were," said El.

"Nope, they didn't," Ida Faye insisted. I had such a good disguise — dressed like a gypsy, don't you know — and I changed my voice. Most of them never caught on!"

"As wicked then as you are now, I see," exclaimed El. "So people really didn't get into crime or anything like that on Halloween?" he continued.

"Well, I do remember at the parade one year, I heard that somebody squirted ink right onto Queen Halloween. I guess you could call that a crime."

"Maybe a shame, Lady, but not a crime," interrupted El.

She thought hard and then commented, "I guess there were a few other things, like about the street car. The last stop of the line was in West End, near Lynchburg College. When the conductor got there, he had to get off and switch the cable so's the car could go the other way, and then he had to turn the seats back, too. On Halloween, some kids would move the cable after the conductor was back on and try to change the seats when he won't looking."

El thought that hardly qualified as a crime, either. Realizing that this could be the basis of information for another assignment, he asked Ida Faye how much it cost to ride the street car. After thinking for a moment, the older lady concluded that it could have been seven cents, and that a weekly pass was no more than fifty cents.

Ida Faye was comparing street cars to modern-day transportation when they arrived at the DMV. "Well, here we are," she exclaimed. "Let's go inside and give you ole Bassy!"

Nobody had ever accused Ida Faye of doing anything public without drawing attention to herself, and today was no different. She approached the clerk with, "Good morning. I am ninety years old, but I won't always old. I don't drive anymore, and I want to give my car to this young man here. He's El, my great-grandson!"

The clerk smiled, and as she processed the title change, she commented on how young Ida Faye looked. This was all the encouragement needed, for Ida Faye expounded on her ailments and then indicated that she still had a good mind. "I'm not like the 75-year-old woman who had a baby," she stated matter-of-factly.

Ida Faye knew that she had hooked the clerk, and so she went on with her story, "When her friends came to see the baby, she wouldn't show it to them. They kept on begging, 'til finally she told them that she couldn't show it to them because she'd forgotten where she put it!"

Bursts of laughter erupted throughout the entire room. El blushed, and as soon as the business was completed, he took Ida Faye's arm and gently pushed her out the front door. He was careful to hold tightly to the car title clutched in his other hand.

On the ride home, El debated with himself about letting Ida Faye know that he would no longer be the one to drive her all over town. He concluded that this was not the right time to tell his great-grandmother, so he put it off one more time. "See you tomorrow," he promised as he pulled the apartment door shut behind him.

Two hours later, Ida Faye was fuming. Jane had phoned to say that she was going off on another weekend trip, and, once again, she would not be able to take her mother with her. No amount of arguing could change her mind. It didn't matter that Ida Faye *wanted* to wait in a hotel room alone while her daughter attended meetings. *Jane always has to hover, just like some damn bird.* Ida Faye whacked at the sofa pillow with her cane. "I wish I could be alive to see her when she's an old woman," she muttered. "She'll find out that most of it is hellish!"

Ida Faye rocked her chair as feverishly as she could manage, punctuating its creaks with snorts and certain obscenities that lay hidden in her mind. Then, with a determined look on the wrinkled face and a devilish glint in the dimming eyes, she steadied herself with her cane and stood up. The old lady loudly announced, as if to an audience, "I won't always old. I don't need her or nobody else to help me. Just you watch!" With that, she hobbled into the bedroom and began to move furniture.

Her body cried out with the pain from all its labors. Ida Faye barely had enough strength to pour herself a bowl of cereal for supper and then get into her pajamas. As she surveyed the results of her struggles, she was pleased with the newly-arranged room and proud of herself, in spite of the toll it had taken. With the bed on this side of the room, the air couldn't blow directly on her arthritic joints as she slept. True, she would no longer be able to reach the phone from her berth, and the emergency house bell was on the opposite wall, yet Ida was satisfied. Besides, she still had her mama's old flatiron on the floor right beside her bed, in case anyone ever attacked her.

Ida Faye managed to stretch herself out on the mattress briefly before a leg cramp hit. She yelled in pain as she tried to move the crippled toes forward to help release the taut muscles. Her thrashing arms hit the bedside lamp and she instinctively tried to save it, flinging herself to the floor and against the protective iron, as she struggled to regain her balance.

The next eight hours were but a fog in her mind. She didn't know how long she lay on the floor, totally enveloped in pain so intense she could not even cry out. When the tears did come, she was only vaguely aware of them; she was certain that she was dying alone. At some point in the dark night she managed to pull a pillow to her chest and cling to it. As she drifted in and out of consciousness, she muttered the numbers that Jane had punched into her telephone memory system, "911."

Her sister found her there the next morning — a cold, crumpled body with just a whisper of life coursing through it. A siren wailed, and out of its sound Ida Faye heard the voice of her dead husband, Elmer. "Hey, Pete," he was saying, "I have old Bassy all gassed up and ready to go. We're gonna take a great trip together, but you first gotta promise not to tell anybody 'bout why I named her that. Will you?"

Ida Faye snickered, "Yeah, I promise. Only you and me will ever know. Nobody ever picked up that I always said 'B-ASSy' nice and slow. I guess they just thought that was the way I talked. But I never forgot them bad words you said that Christmas morning 'cause you couldn't get the fire started. You was standing there in your underdrawers, just freezing. You always prided yourself on how fast you could build a fire in the old 'heatrola.' You didn't know I was anywhere around. All of a sudden you slammed that stove door and let out, 'Bear's Ass, Bear's Ass, Bear's Ass!' I thought I'd die laughing. If we could've afforded a car that year, you sure won't have agreed to name it B-ASSy."

The ambulance attendant noted the trace of a smile on the wrinkled face. As he bent his head close to the lips, he thought she spoke the name "Elmer." The breathing stopped, and he signaled to the driver to turn off the siren.

El insisted that he be allowed to drive Bassy at the front of the funeral procession. He argued, "The car is like a member of the family. I never did find out why she called it Bassy, but I suspect it had a special, intimate meaning for Ida Faye and my great-granddaddy. She promised to tell me, but then she never expected this crazy accident to happen."

He continued, "When I drove the car to school and showed it to my writing class, they acted like I had brought an old friend. Everybody wanted to have a group picture taken with the car — haven't even had it developed yet.

They're all going to be sad to hear that Lady's gone, and I won't have anymore of her stories to tell." El silently breathed a prayer of thanks that he had not broken the news to Ida about his plans to quit being her "sho-fer."

The daughters had Ida Faye laid out in her favorite — a pink, ruffled dress. The snowy white hair curled in soft waves against the quilted interior, her fingernails matched the dress, and Ida Faye Crawford appeared to be much younger than her age. The make-up artist who prepared her body must have seen the beauty of years past and succumbed to the charm of this amazing woman, even as she lay silent and cold.

The minister labeled her as a person of great faith and vitality, "who loved a good fight." He read from the twenty-third Psalm and paused, to re-read, "My cup runneth over." "Ida Faye's life has attested to her belief in this verse," he proclaimed, and the mourners nodded. As the soloist sang, "There is a place of quiet rest, near to the heart of God," Jane wondered how that would set with her mother and smiled through her tears. Annie kept her arm tight around El's trembling shoulders. One grandson summarized his feelings in the note attached to red roses, "I'm gonna miss that wildcat!"

The family called the trip to the cemetery, "Lady's Parade." It seemed appropriate. El drove Bassy to lead the procession, and as the entourage moved through the streets, El could almost hear Lady's voice, "Look in there and take out just one thing. Don't matter what it is, 'cause before we're through I'll tell you a story about every last thing in that box." He reached over and touched the embossed box and realized that it was empty.